# Tomb of Brain Ooze

## by M. D. Payne

Grosset & Dunlap
An Imprint of Penguin Group (USA) LLC

To my editor, Rob, for keeping the Juices flowing

GROSSET & DUNLAP
Published by the Penguin Group
Penguin Group (USA) LLC, 375 Hudson Street, New York, New York 10014, USA

USA | Canada | UK | Ireland | Australia | New Zealand | India | South Africa | China

penguin.com
A Penguin Random House Company

Cover illustrated by Keith Zoo.

*Library of Congress Cataloging-in-Publication Data is available.*

ISBN 978-0-448-48200-2                    10 9 8 7 6 5 4 3 2 1

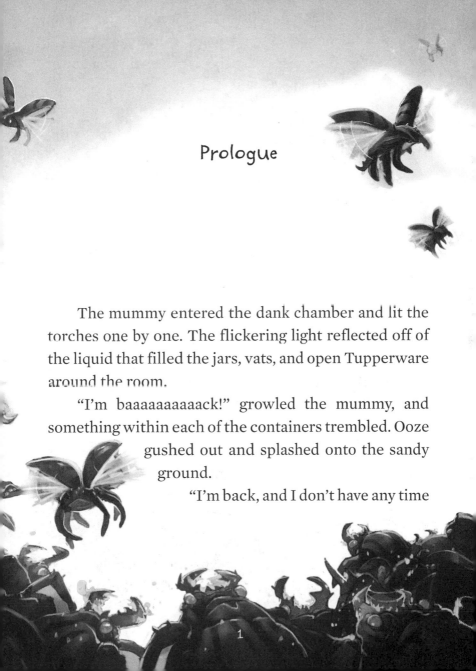

# Prologue

The mummy entered the dank chamber and lit the torches one by one. The flickering light reflected off of the liquid that filled the jars, vats, and open Tupperware around the room.

"I'm baaaaaaaaaack!" growled the mummy, and something within each of the containers trembled. Ooze gushed out and splashed onto the sandy ground.

"I'm back, and I don't have any time

for chitchat," said the mummy. He clapped his hands twice, and a fine white dust flew from his bandages. "We've got to get down to business straight away."

Two figures appeared in the doorway that had been chiseled through a rock wall. They crouched down low to get through the doorway without harming their bird heads. Their beaks clicked as they bowed low to the mummy.

"Yes, yes, do come in," he said. "Make it snappy— we've got a lot of prep work to do."

The bird-heads went back through the doorway, and returned quickly with another mummy. This one was motionless as they carried it into the room. They bowed again and dropped it at the feet of the first mummy, who was alive and very impatient.

"All right, all right," he said, snapping his fingers. "Enough ceremony. Stop bowing and give me the Blade of a Thousand and One Souls already!"

The bird-heads clicked their beaks in anger, but obeyed. One reached behind its back and unsheathed a long, curved blade that started narrow near the hilt and widened toward the point. Before the bird-head could bow and present it to the mummy, the mummy snatched it away.

"SQUAWK!" yelled the bird-head.

"Get outta here!" yelled the mummy in reply.

They held up their hands in protest, clicked their

beaks, and hissed, but backed out.

Once they were gone, the mummy turned his attention back to the containers.

"Now . . . ," he said, swinging the sword carelessly with one hand while searching around the chamber. "Where are you, Tutankhamen? Tonight your body shall burn to feed your brain."

He strolled around, peering into jugs, lifting up the larger Tupperware containers and peering underneath, making sure not to spill the precious juices on his head.

Finally, he came to a laundry basket lined with a trash bag.

"Aha!"

He plunged his hand into the ooze and pulled out a pulsating brain.

"Tutankhamen!" he screeched. "I. Can't. WAIT. To eat you!" He held the brain up high. "So young. So fresh. With the exception of our new visitors', your brains will be the richest. Your brains will take me *soooo* many places—deep into so many minds!"

The brain squirted a purplish-black goo directly into the eyes of the mummy.

"WARGH!" he yelled, dropping the brain— SPLUNK—and the sword—CLANK.

He used the bandages on his hands to clean his eyes. Once he opened them again, he gasped and pointed at the brain.

"Nooooo!" he yelled. "Look what you've done to yourself."

The brain was starting to disintegrate into the sand. The mummy picked it up, blew off all the sand that he could, and then plopped it back into the trash-bag-lined laundry basket with a PLOOOP.

"How dare you disobey your master on a night such as this?!" he yelled, picking up the sword. "Tonight of all nights! YOUR night. The night that has been thousands of years in the making. The night we will drive what's left of your spirit from your body and back into your MIND!"

The angry mummy raised the sword high and brought it down onto the lifeless mummy in the sand. FWACK. The head rolled into a corner. FWACK, FWACK! No more arms. FWACK, FWACK!

"How does that feel, Tut?" screeched the mummy.

"Noooooooo!" yelled the dusty old head on the ground. "What you're doing is wrong, and the spirits shall make you pay."

"Zip it, Tut," said the mummy. "I didn't actually need you to answer. It was a rhetorical question!"

FWACK, FWACK, FWACK!!!

The mummy went on and on, until Tutankhamen's body was just a pile of parts. He gathered up all of the parts and placed them in the center of the room. Then he grabbed Tutankhamen's head and held it so that his eyes pointed at the pile.

"Take a good look!" said the mummy. "It will surely be your last."

With his other hand, the mummy grabbed one of the torches from the wall and threw it on the pile.

SCHWWOOOOOF!

Tutankhamen's body parts caught on fire almost immediately.

"Nooooooooo," screeched the head. The laundry basket began to bubble and froth in anger.

"AMAN-RA!" boomed the mummy, holding Tutankhamen's head high.

An eerie purple glow filled the room. The flames danced around Tutankhamen's parts like orange and purple snakes. The body crackled and snapped, and the pieces started folding into one another and sent sparks to the very top of the chamber. Then the sparks blew back down, hitting the liquid in the vats and containers with little hisses. Before the fire got too low, the mummy threw Tutankhamen's head on the very top.

"Sizzle, sizzle!" the mummy yelled.

"You. Will. PAY!" said Tutankhamen's head on top of the flaming pile, his mouth opening wide with a CRACKLE.

The mummy pulled out a vial from somewhere in his wrappings, popped out the stopper, took a mouthful, and blew the liquid over the burning pile.

"ANUBIS-DUN!" the mummy yelled.

There was a low moan, and then, POP-POP, both of Tutankhamen's eyes exploded juicily.

The fire died down quickly, and with a POOF, a large cloud of purple and red sparks swirled, gathered, and tumbled into the laundry basket.

The mummy peered into the basket and, with a grin, said, "Yes. YESSS. Glow with your newfound powers. GLOW. And grow. I'll be back to eat every last bit of you, you false king. You and all those who came before you. And after."

A large scarab beetle scampered into the room and stopped at the feet of the mummy. The mummy raised his sword high once again and chopped off the scarab's head. He leaned down, picked up the body, and tipped its oozing green fluid into his mouth.

SLLLLLUUUUUUUURP!

He dropped the shell and sword and flexed his muscles.

"I am the only ruler now!" he yelled. "Now . . . who's next?"

# The Burpstronauts Return

"So what was your favorite part of the trip?" Shane asked as Gordon and I looked through the small porthole of Murrayhotep's spaceship.

The spaceship whirred and hummed with a deep throbbing BWOOOW-BWOOOW as it made its way to Earth.

"I think my favorite part was when the moon ate Zorflogg!" said Ben. "MUNCH, BURP, Earth saved!"

"And not a moment too soon," said Shane, carefully high-fiving Ben so the zero gravity wouldn't push them apart. "We were almost space junk. What about you, Chris? What was your favorite part?"

"Just being on the moon," I replied, sighing. My breath pushed me away from the porthole.

"Don't sigh too hard, Space Boy," said Gordon, catching me before I floated all the way into the control panel. "If you crash into that control panel, we'll all be lost. And I don't know about you, but I can't wait to get home."

I stared at the control panel, and absolutely nothing made sense to me.

"I'm still trying to figure out how a stinky, grumpy old mummy got his own spaceship," said Nabila as she floated over to the control panel to take a closer look. "And something about these controls doesn't feel right."

"What do you mean?" asked Ben, floating toward her. He misfired and slammed his head against her butt.

"Wah?!!" she said.

"PDA! PDA!" yelled Gordon. "Quit it, you lovebirds. Just because you're going out doesn't mean we have to see your bizarre dating rituals."

Nabila's cheeks turned red as she tried to ignore an obviously grumpy Gordon.

"Well, these controls are labeled with a variation of hieroglyphic writing," she continued, "but it seems to be fashioned in some sort of code."

"Oh, I thought you were Little Miss Egyptian Know-It-All!" Gordon said, laughing.

"Stop it, Gordon," Shane said.

I looked over at Gordon. "Just because I, yes, I, the nerdiest kid you know except for Ben, beat you at moon football doesn't mean you can take it out on everyone else," I said.

"Sorry," said Gordon. "I miss *real* football, and I'm tired of missing so many practices, and I'm just . . . tired. Is there anywhere to take a nap on this thing?"

"We're all exhausted," I said. "But we'll have plenty of time to sleep once we're back on Earth."

"Maybe we can ask Director Z and Lunch Lady to erase our parents' minds for another week," Shane added.

"That would be sweeeeeet," said Gordon. "Don't they have to listen to you now that you're a Director?"

"The only people I can control with my pendant are the monsters," I replied.

"Which reminds me," said Gordon, "where is this pendant that you keep talking about?"

"It's a secret I keep deep inside of me," I said.

Shane snickered, knowing exactly where I kept the pendant.

Ben had finally rotated so he was face-to-face with Nabila, and the two of them stared at the controls.

"Director Z figured out how to work the ship," said Ben. "I'm sure we can, as well."

"But Director Z only figured out what one button did before sending us back to Earth," Nabila said, and pointed to the tattered piece of tape above a big red button. AUTOPILOT was scribbled on the tape in huge black letters.

"Ah," said Ben. "I see."

"I'm going to see if I can crack the code," she said.

Nabila whipped a notebook out of her fluorescent pink fanny pack without thinking about the lack of gravity. Plastic baggies, pencils, pens, erasers, even Ben's motion-sickness pills spilled out, and everything flew around the bridge of Murrayhotep's ship.

"Where's the kitchen sink?" asked Shane.

"Don't lose those pills, or I'm gonna lose my lunch," said Ben.

"Yeah, get 'em," I said. "Remember what happened on the way up to the moon?"

"I think I still have some of the chunks in my hair," said Gordon. "Blech."

We struggled to get everything that was floating around the slick black bridge, and Nabila stuffed it all back into her fanny pack.

"Now, what was I doing?" she asked.

"Decoding hieroglyphs," said Ben as he handed Nabila a pencil.

"Aww, thanks, *habibi*," replied Nabila. She giggled a little.

Shane clamped Gordon's mouth shut before he could say anything.

"I wish I could tell other kids at school that I was actually there," I said. "On the moon!"

"Which brings me to *my* favorite part," Shane said. "I'm glad that I was able to see you on the moon. Chris Taylor, my best friend, on the moon—now that's somethin' special! My only regret is that I didn't try out any karate moves as a vampire on the moon. What was I thinking?"

I stared dreamily at the blue planet as it crept closer into view.

"Hey, I wonder where Director Z and the monsters are," I said, smooshing my face up against the glass to see if I could spot the other, Victorian-era spaceship.

"I'm sure they're fine," said Gordon. "That busted old ship is just perfect for transporting busted old monsters. I'll take the modern comforts of Murrayhotep's ship over that any day."

"The monsters are actually not that busted or old anymore," said Shane. "The moon juiced them up pretty good."

"Maybe Director Z will let us keep this spaceship," I said. "Once Nabila cracks the code, the universe is ours."

"Yeah!" said Ben. "Let me just grab a ten-year supply of motion-sickness pills back home, and then I'm ready!"

"You guys do whatever you want, but drop me off first," said Gordon. "We've been away for almost a week! Between the zero-g and monster-juice-drinking, my muscles are shrinking, and I'm no longer the greatest athlete in the history of Rio Vista Middle School."

"Well, you won't have to drink monster juice ever again," said Ben. "That was a one-time-only deal. Too bad drinking it a second time would kill us. It was pretty awesome. The best cure for nausea I've ever had."

Everyone nodded. Everyone but Gordon.

"Sure, it's all just one nonstop monster party for you guys," said Gordon. "But I still have killer indigestion."

"Get ready to stop complaining, Gordon," I said, turning away from the porthole. "We're almost home! We should probably strap ourselves down or something."

As we floated down to the chairs, the lights turned red in the cabin, and an alarm sounded.

"Hey, wait, what's going on?" I yelled over the alarm.

A button on the massive control panel started blinking crazily. Nabila and I floated over to it.

"I know you haven't had much time, but did you figure out any of this?" I asked.

"Barely," she said. She looked back and forth from her notepad to the hieroglyph above the button. "Based

12

on what I've worked out, this could be either 'Space Door' or 'Monkey Pie.'"

"Something tells me it's not 'Monkey Pie,'" Ben said.

"You can never be sure with these types of things," said Shane.

"So, 'Space Door,'" Nabila said, ignoring Shane. "Assuming my previous translations are correct, of course."

"Space Door . . . ," I repeated, trying to figure out what it meant.

"Air lock!" she and I shouted at the same time.

The throbbing of the ship slowed down until it stopped.

The lights on the control panel flickered . . .

BLLLLRRRZZZZZP!

. . . and then went out.

"What's going on?" Gordon asked.

"The air lock!" Nabila yelled. "Someone—or something—stopped the ship and opened the air lock!"

"WHAT?!" Gordon yelled. "To get into the ship?"

"Only one way to find out," said Shane, and he headed to the back of the ship, where the air lock was located.

We all followed him. Halfway to the back of the ship all of the lights went out.

"Nooooooo!" screeched Nabila.

"Oof," said Shane as I elbowed him in the eye.

"Sorry," I said.

"What's going on?" said Ben with a trembling voice.

With a great WHOOOSH, a dark figure flew past us toward the cabin.

"Who is it?" I asked. "Twenty-Three, are you playing a joke on us? Ha-ha-ha!"

In the pale blue light, I could see a figure floating over the controls. It was far too big to be Twenty-Three.

"Who is that?" asked Nabila.

Before I could figure out who or what it was, the portholes were sealed with a metallic SCRAAAAPE and an alarm sounded.

BIP, BOOP, BEEP!

Rockets fired, and we were pushed deep into the back of the ship.

"What's going on?" said Gordon.

"Someone's hijacked the ship!" I yelled. "And we're heading to Earth fast!"

Now the BWOOOW-BWOOOW of the ship amped up into a SCREEEEEEEE as the ship hit the atmosphere.

"Hold on!" I said.

"To what?!" screeched Nabila.

"Something," I yelled. "Anything!"

SCREEEEEEEEEEEEEEEEEEEEE—

BOOOOM!

# Dank and Dark

The next thing I remember was waking up with my face in the sand.

"Blech!" I yelled, spitting the sand out of my mouth and trying to clear it away from my eyes so I could see.

"Shane?" I asked. "Gordon? Are we back on Paradise Island? Why is the beach so cold? This sand tastes like dog breath."

I heaved a little as some of the sand went down the back of my throat.

HWWWWARF!

I held back my barf and opened my eyes . . .

It was pitch-black.

We were definitely not on Paradise Island.

"Guys?" I said.

There was an echo, and for a minute, all I could hear was my voice bouncing around.

"So I'm in a room filled with sand?" I asked out loud. "*We're* in a room? Guys?!"

The silence was insane. I could hear my heartbeat throb through my body.

"I've got to keep calm," I said. "I can't freak out."

Lifting up my head, and then my body, I stood in the cold sand. It was hard to stand up straight; I was so dizzy, and it was so dark.

I slowly raised my hand in front of me, but couldn't even see it in front of my face.

Something pinched my arm.

"WAH!" I yelled, and jumped away from whatever was there, tumbling back down.

"It's just me," said Shane. "Sorry I scared you."

Shane awkwardly helped me up. His sandy hand gripped my sandy arm. I couldn't see him, but I pictured him as a huge sand monster. And I could hear him breathing loudly. I could even smell him . . . or was it the sand?

"I can't believe I didn't smell you there before," I said, shocked.

"What?" he asked.

"Never mind," I said. "Where are we? And how are we not on the ship anymore?"

"Maybe we *are* on the ship?" asked Shane. "It slammed into the Earth, cracked open, and filled with sand?"

"BLLLLLOOOOORRRGGPPPPPHHH!"

"What's that? A sand monster?" Shane asked, gripping my arm.

"I'm not a sand monster!" Gordon said, coughing. "But I did just barf up a mouthful of sand."

"I'm glad I couldn't see that," I said.

"Oh, you guys are blind, too?" Gordon asked.

"Blind?!" I screeched. "Oh man . . . what if we're blind?"

"Then we'll learn how to drive a car like Ray Charles," said Shane. "Cool."

"Who has light?" I asked. "Did anyone's phone survive the trip to the moon?"

"Nope," said Gordon. "Where are Ben and Nabila? Where are we? Aw, man, we were supposed to be home already. I think I'm going to miss hockey tryouts. Arrrgh!"

"Ben?!" I yelled. "Nabila?"

My voice bounced around for a minute, and then there was nothing but the sound of our breathing.

"Get down and crawl around," said Shane. "Maybe we'll find them."

The three of us got down on our hands and knees.

"Okay," I said. "Let's all head out in opposite directions."

We turned around awkwardly and began to crawl through the moist, smelly sand.

"This was easier when we had monsters who could see in the dark to guide us," I said.

"Who knows," said Shane. "There might be some monsters in here who can see in the dark."

"Something tells me they won't help us," I said.

"Oh, I've got someone!" yelled Gordon.

"Who is it?" I asked.

"Hold on, I'm feeling the face," said Gordon. "Glasses. Thick. It's Nabila. Nabila, wake up."

Shane and I stopped while Gordon tried to wake up Nabila.

"Is she okay?" I asked. "Check for blood."

"Ben might want to put his hands all over her," said Gordon. "But I don't."

"What are you, six years old?" I said. "Don't be all weird about it. At least check to see if she's breathing."

There was a long pause, and then Gordon said, "Yeah, she's breathing!"

"All right, let's find Ben," I said, and we kept crawling ahead.

There was a dull thump.

"OW!" yelled Shane.

"What is it?" Gordon and I asked at the same time.

"I hit my head on a wall," said Shane.

"Great!" I said. "I was worried this room would go on forever."

"I don't think it's a room," said Shane. "It feels like rock. I think we're in a cave."

"That would explain the sand," said Gordon.

"Can you crawl around the edges so we know how big it is?" I asked. "Maybe find if there's a way out?"

"Got it," said Shane.

The sand got colder as I moved farther from my friends.

Suddenly, my hand came down on a sweaty forehead.

"Ben?" I asked. "Ben?!"

There was no response. I leaned in to see if I could hear Ben breathing. As I moved my ear closer and closer to his mouth, I could hear the muffled sound of air gurgling through something wet. Inching closer, I lost track of distance and ended up sticking my ear right into something slimy, cold, and moist.

"Yuck!" I yelled, touching the side of my ear.

Without thinking, I sniffed my fingers.

"Barf!" I yelled.

"He must have found Ben," said Shane and Gordon.

"Is he okay?" asked Shane.

"I think so," I said. "It's so hard to tell."

"Good," said Shane. "At least we're all here."

"Gordon, bring Nabila over here," I said. "Let's stay together."

Gordon dragged Nabila over and with an OOOF dropped down in the sand next to me.

"I made it all the way around the cave and couldn't find any way out," Shane said.

"How do you know you made it all the way around?" I asked.

"Echolocation," Shane said. "Like a bat."

"Is that some leftover monster power?!" I shouted. "Can you use it to get us out of here?!"

"Just kidding," he said. "I plopped my shoe down, and then when I found it again, I knew that I had made it all the way around. It's not a very big cave."

"What if you hadn't come back to your shoe?" asked Gordon. "You'd be blind, in a cave, AND without a shoe."

"We're not blind!" I yelled.

"Now what?" Gordon asked. "I'm getting exhausted dragging people through the dark. Lucky sacks of potatoes are just sleeping."

"Maybe that's what we should do," said Shane, crawling over to us.

"That's not such a bad idea," I said. "We can't get out, so what can get in? I haven't slept since before the moon. Except for being unconscious, which wasn't very refreshing."

"Awesome," said Gordon, and immediately began snoring.

I plunked my head down in the sand and sighed.

"Oh, that funky sand does feel good," said Shane.

Gordon's snore suddenly took on a funny scraping sound.

SHICK SHICK SHICK!

"Is he okay?" I asked.

"I don't think that's him," said Shane.

"What do you mean?" I asked.

But then I heard it. A nerve-racking scuttling sound.

CHICKA, CHATTER, SKITTER!

And it was getting closer.

## Cave Monsters
## of the Deep

We could still see nothing, but the skittering sound quickly got closer.

"AHH, get them off me!" shrieked Nabila, suddenly awake.

"Hey! That tickles," giggled Ben in his sleep. "Tee-hee. Stop it."

"What tickles?" I asked. "What's on you?"

Ben didn't answer. But he didn't

need to. Suddenly several of "them" were on my legs and crawling up my jeans.

"Oh man, what's on me?!" yelled Shane. "They're so fast!"

"Nabila!" I screeched, pushing the hard-shelled, chattering creatures off of my lap and away from my belly. "Do you have a flashlight in your fanny pack?"

"No . . . AHH!" she screeched in return. "But I do have matches . . . AHH! They're starting to bite!"

I could hear Nabila get up and run.

"OOOOOOOF!"

"Nabila!" yelled Shane.

"I hit a wall," she said. "My fanny pack just came unclasped! I can't get to my . . . OW!"

"Ah, my finger!" yelled Shane. "I can't brush them off fast enough!"

I felt two bites at once on each thigh.

"Ouuuuuuch!" I yelled, jumping up and pushing the skittering things back down to the ground. "We've got to help Nabila!"

"I don't even know which way I'm facing!" yelled Gordon.

In the dark, I ran as fast as I could toward Nabila's screams . . . and hit a wall.

CRUNCH!

The impact crushed some of the scratching, biting creatures that were crawling all over me. I bounced off of the wall and right onto another pile of moving, hissing, scraping shells.

"Throw yourself against the walls!" I yelled. "Crush these nasties!"

I ran back to the wall and slammed up against it again, this time pushing really hard. The scampering creatures poked into me as they crushed and crunched.

CRUNCH CRUNCH CRUNCH!

"I hope my shirt is wet from their blood and not mine," said Shane. I still couldn't see him, but he was nearby and crunching more of the skittering creatures.

CRUNCH CRUNCH CRUNCH!

"What are they?" I asked. "Crabs? Bugs? I wish we could see!"

"Are they sussuroblats?" asked Gordon.

"They'd have to be really small," said Shane. "And they don't smell like it."

"Nabila, can you throw a spell at them or something?" I said. "Like you did back in Gallow Manor with Murrayhotep?"

"I don't even know what we're dealing with!" she shrieked. "If this isn't some sort of Egyptian evil, nothing is going to happen! Let's just find my fanny pack."

I felt my way down the wall to Nabila and grabbed her by the shoulders. "Where did you lose it?"

"I'm not sure," she said. "OUCH! My knee!"

I swatted at her knee and caught another shell.

"It's hard to do anything while we're jumping around like we have ants in our pants," I said. "We need to let them bite until we find the fanny pack."

"There's one in my pants!" yelled Shane. "I don't think letting them bite is the best plan!"

"I found it. I've got the fanny pack!" yelled Gordon. "Gahhhh! They're swarming all over it and trying to pull it away."

"Well, TRY something, Nabila!" I yelled as one of the hard creatures tried to crawl into my T-shirt. Its sharp feet dug into my belly. "A 'get away' spell or something!"

"OSIRIS-MUN-RA!" she chanted.

For a moment, there was silence, and the creepy creatures dropped off of me.

"It's working!" said Gordon. "I've got it!"

"I'm over here," said Nabila. "Over here, over here!"

Suddenly, there was a flash as Nabila lit a match.

"Ouch," I yelled, holding up my hand. "It's so bright."

"We've been in the dark so long," said Shane.

I looked around for a few seconds to get my bearings, and my mouth popped open.

"The entire room is filled with them," said Gordon.

We were surrounded by . . .

"Scarabs," said Nabila. "Scarab beetles. That's why the spell worked. They must be under some sort of Egyptian enchantment."

They slowly backed away from the flame, piling up

on one another. We had ended up in the center of the cave. In one corner, Ben was still passed out. The scarabs that ran away from the flame headed toward him.

We were drowning in a sea of scarabs.

"Ben!" yelled Nabila. "Wake up! OW!"

Nabila flung the match to the ground as it burned down to her finger.

In the dark, I could hear Shane rush over to Ben, crunching on shells as he went.

"BEN?!" Shane yelled. "Ben?! Wake up NOW!"

SLAP! SLAP! SLAP!

Shane slapped Ben's cheeks, and I could hear moans, followed by . . .

"What's on me, Shane?" yelled Ben. "Get them off me!"

Nabila lit another match as Shane helped Ben up. "Another spell!" I yelled to Nabila, running closer to her and the flame while trying to scrape the scarabs off of me. "Quick!"

"Another spell won't matter," she said, looking around frantically. "We've got to drive them out of here, not just hold them back. We need to find something to burn. They'll run from flames, but we need something BIG."

"Over there," I yelled. "There's a mummy in a chair!"

"I'm glad I didn't crawl over him in the dark," said Shane, running over with Ben.

"Hurry!" she said. "The wrappings! This is my last match!"

"What?!" I screeched. "Who packs two matches?!"

"Gordon, help us out," Shane said. "Let's unwrap from the head down—slowly! Let's keep the wrapping intact."

I ignored the scarabs biting deeply into my legs and grabbed Nabila's fanny pack. Pulling out her notebook, I ripped out the first page I could grab hold of.

"Those are my notes on the hieroglyph code!" she yelled.

"No time!" I yelled, watching the flame of her match get dangerously close to her finger.

"OW," she yelled.

"Hold it, hold it!" I said.

I crumpled up the paper and threw it on the ground.

"Drop it," I said, and she dropped the match.

There was a moment of darkness, and then something glowed inside the paper. The paper caught fire quickly.

"Shane?" I yelled.

"We're on it," he said, and came back with a large pile of mummy wrappings. He pulled one out and dangled it over the paper just as it was going out. The flame transferred to the wrapping. He quickly put the rest on the fire.

An orange glow filled the room, and the scarabs

dropped off—and out of—our pants. They chattered nervously, but stayed in the cave.

Gordon jumped over to a moldy old wooden box, quickly kicked it into pieces, and dragged them over. Once those were on the fire, the flames really got going, and the scarabs finally gave up.

In a giant mass they hurried toward the wall and burrowed into the sand.

SCHHHRP SCHHHHRP SCHHHHRP!

And then silence.

"Scarabs are all over the world, but there's only one place that has mummies hiding deep in sandy caves. I'm pretty sure I know where we are . . . ," Nabila said.

"Egypt," we all said in unison.

## Follow the Scarabs . . .

The fire continued to burn in the cave prison. The only sign of the scarab infestation that had just plagued us was the holes in our jeans. We sat around the fire for a few minutes, too tired to talk.

"At least we know *he's* still around," said Shane, breaking the silence.

"Who?" I asked.

"Murray," said Shane. "I was worried about him. Looks like he made it."

"Yes, it was clearly Murrayhotep who hijacked our ship," said Nabila. "We're most likely in a tomb or a pyramid. The scarabs. The mummy. The fact that my spell worked."

"Yay for Hotep," mumbled Gordon.

"Yay for him," I said. "Not so 'yay' for us."

"We gotta get out of here," said Ben. "We're gonna get cursed."

"There's no such thing as curses," I said to Nabila. "Right?"

"A three-thousand-year-old mummy crash-landed our spaceship and trapped us in a dark hole with hungry scarabs," replied Nabila. "I'd say we're already cursed."

"Curses!" Ben yelled with a British accent, and shook his fist in the air.

"Ahem," someone said.

"Who was that?" asked Ben.

"It's quite drafty in here," said the voice. "So drafty, in fact, that I believe you've woken me from my slumber."

"It's the mummy," said Gordon, pointing. "The shirtless mummy in the chair."

Shane, Gordon, and Ben had unwrapped the mummy all the way down to his waist. His skin, blackened and tough from being mummified, was exposed all the way up to his head.

"Oops," said Shane. "Sorry about that."

"No, that's quite all right," said the mummy. "I don't

think I've been awake in . . . well . . . what year is it?"

"2014," I said.

"Has it been that long?" the mummy said, yawning. He stretched, and his bones cracked and creaked. "My, my. It's been just under a millennium since I last woke."

"What's your name?" I asked.

"I'm Neferkare," he replied. "Pleasure to meet you."

"What are you doing in here?" I asked. "Where are we?"

"It's been so long, I don't even remember," said Neferkare. "I believe we're deep below a pyramid." He looked far off into space as if trying to remember something. "Or is it just a tomb . . . on the Nile? In the Valley of the Kings in Upper Egypt? I can't remember."

"But we are in Egypt?" asked Nabila.

"Yes, young lady, we indeed are," he said, yawning once again. "A land that I once ruled. And now it seems it will soon rise again, although this time as an evil empire, with Murray as the all-powerful pharaoh . . ."

He cocked his head and stared at Nabila.

"My, what wonderful eyes you have. They look so beautiful . . . so familiar . . ."

"Oh, thanks," said Nabila. She giggled nervously.

"Murray?" Shane asked. "You know Murray?"

"I do indeed," said Neferkare. "It is he who has trapped me eternally in this place, though I would rather be trapped in this dank, dark room than suffer what he had in mind for me."

"I have so many questions," said Shane. "But I have to ask one right away—is his name really Murray?"

"Indeed," said Neferkare.

"For reals?" said Shane.

"I'm not exactly sure what 'for reals' means," said Neferkare. "But I'm going to say yes, for reals."

"I always thought he made that up," said Shane. He looked up into the air, perplexed.

Our fire was beginning to die down.

"We have more important questions," I said, walking up to the mummy. "And we don't have much time. Neferkare, please tell us—what is Murray's plan?"

"The details are sketchy, but in short, he began secretly collecting the brains of pharaohs—the kings and queens of Egypt—before they were to be mummified. Many here believe the brain is garbage, to be thrown out during the mummification process. But Murray wanted them for some reason. When my turn came to have my brain collected, I convinced Murray that my brain was of no use to him. He had so many, he didn't seem to care. So here I sit in my old chair, snoozing away eternity."

Neferkare stood up from his chair and began to walk toward where the scarabs had dived into the sand.

"Wait!" I said. "What are you doing?"

"I'm very, very tired," said Neferkare. "I was already

one hundred years old when I was mummified. With my brain still in place, I find that I can't stop thinking when I'm awake. And I must go back to sleep. But I can't do so without fresh wrappings. I will search this pyramid, find what I need, wrap myself up, and then go back to sleep."

"How are you going to get out of this room?" Gordon asked.

"Lucky for us," said Neferkare, "the scarabs were hungry. They arrived one by one, popping up in the sand, but when you scared them with the fire, they headed back in a pack—a huge pack large enough to create a tunnel underneath this room and, hopefully, into the main hallways of the pyramid. Follow me."

"Why would you come back to this prison?" I asked. "Come with us—help us find a way out."

"Yeah," Shane said. "You can come home with us. We're short one mummy at the moment."

"No, I must come back," said Neferkare. "I would never leave were it not for the need for new wrappings. I'm just hoping Murray doesn't see me. I think he's forgotten about me, and I'm happy in my tomb."

"What about the scarabs?" Shane asked.

"They will be back. But I'm far too dry for their liking. Murray is a fool for letting them feast on you. But if you can't find your way out of the pyramid—and I don't think you will—you should seriously think about letting the scarabs eat you. It's a far better fate than the one Murray has in store for you."

Neferkare dropped to the sand and began to dig.

"Wait, what fate does Murray have in store for us?" I asked.

"Well, we should get going!" said Neferkare, ignoring my question. "Remember, don't breathe in the sand, and keep pushing!"

He disappeared into the sand.

## Sand-Swimming

After the mummy's bandaged feet wiggled their way into the ground, the rest of the sand in the dank, dark cave began to shift. I could hear the chattering of the scarabs from underneath.

"Are you sure this is safe?" Ben asked. "Those creepy-crawlies don't seem that far off."

"There's only one way to find out!" I yelled. "And remember what the mummy said—don't breathe in the sand, and keep pushing."

I took a big breath, dove in headfirst, and pushed my way forward.

I pushed and pushed and pushed. I kept pushing. My chest was about to burst.

*Great,* I thought. *This is going to be the way I die. Why did I listen to the crazy old mummy?*

I had to force myself not to breathe in the sand. I was starting to panic, and I could see stars appearing behind my eyelids. I needed air.

*Just push,* I thought. *Just push.*

I pushed and pushed and pushed until my body couldn't take it anymore. I drew in one breath . . .

HWACK!

. . . and began choking on sand.

My eyes watered, and my brain panicked. My arms flailed—and burst out into the open air!

Something grabbed them and pulled me out. I hacked and threw up some sandy barf.

HWWWWWAAARF!

"Good man," said Neferkare. "The inexperienced always take a little bit longer. I'd wait here for your friends. They'll need your help."

I looked around through watery eyes to see that I was in a large hallway. It was narrow, with jagged, rocky walls, but with a ceiling higher than the one in the dank dungeon we were just in. There were torches up and down the hallway.

A pair of hands burst out of the sand and waved.

I was still recovering from my journey, but the mummy said, "Go on, then!" and pointed at the hands in the sand.

I hacked one more sand ball onto the ground, grabbed the hands, and pulled as hard as I could.

"Good man," repeated Neferkare.

"Wait!" I said as I pulled Shane out of the sand. "You never said what fate Murray has in store for us."

"Yeah." Shane coughed.

"It will take too long to explain," said Neferkare. "You'll find out soon enough. Now, which way to the mummification chamber . . ."

"But how do we get out of here?" I asked as he turned away.

"Yeah," Shane said.

"You okay?" I asked Shane.

"Yeah." Shane coughed once more. He put a finger over one nostril and blew out the sandiest snot rocket ever known to man.

"Whoa," I said.

Suddenly more arms were flailing out of the sand. Exhausted, I pointed at Shane to take care of them. He pulled out a coughing Gordon.

"I have no idea how to leave this place," said Neferkare, slowly shuffling down the hallway. "I'd never care to leave—why would I know how to get out? I'm resigned to my fate. I've gone from being the King of Egypt to the King of Sleep—and I love it."

"That's it?!" I asked. "That's all the advice we get?"

Another pair of hands appeared at the sandy hole.

"Just enjoy your last moments on earth here," said Neferkare as he walked away. "Although Murray craves power, he does not crave wealth. As such, the burial sites in this tomb have not been plundered. Enjoy the gold. Take company with the mummified cats. Maybe you can hide deep enough in the pyramid that Murray won't find you."

"Is there any food?" I asked Neferkare. But he was too far down the hallway to hear me. He slunk into the shadows and was gone.

Shane pulled out Nabila and then went back to slapping a coughing Gordon.

"Try blowing a snot rocket," I said to Gordon.

"Where's"—COUGH—"Ben?"—COUGH—asked Nabila. "He was right behind me!"

I dug into the sand we had crawled through, but Ben was nowhere to be found.

"He's not here," I said.

"He had just grabbed my legs," said Nabila. "He should be here by now!"

"I'll get him," said Shane. "He can't be in too deep."

Shane dove back into the sand, digging like a madman. I tried to hold on to his feet as he disappeared into the sand, but he just kept on going.

It was deathly silent in the hallway. In the direction opposite of where Neferkare had headed, the echo of a SQUAWK met our ears.

"What is that?" asked Nabila. "A bird?"

The squawks got closer. We couldn't just stand there anymore.

"We need to take cover," said Gordon.

"But where?" asked Nabila.

"Any way but that way," I said, pointing toward the squawks.

"What about Ben?" hissed Nabila.

SQUAWK!

"We'll just have to trust that Shane gets him and brings him up at the right time," I said. "We have to go. We have to find somewhere to hide. NOW!"

I grabbed Nabila, and we ran down the hallway and into the first room we could find. Gordon followed. We found ourselves in a large room the same size as the cavern we had come from, but with stone floors, finished walls, and a huge treasure chest in the center.

"What's that?" asked Gordon as I tried to get it open.

A SQUAWK floated into the air.

"I don't care what it is," I said. "It's big enough for us all to hide inside!"

I was eventually able to pry open the huge trunk. Gold coins and jeweled chalices glowed inside. We jumped into the trunk and then pulled down the lid with a CLANK. The light from a nearby torch made its way into the trunk through the hinges.

We could hear the strange SQUAWKs pass by.

"Whoa," said Gordon. "I know that it's dark and all—but how cool is it that we're totally swimming in treasure?"

"Shhhh!" I scolded Gordon. "Wait until they're gone. Enjoy the gold silently."

We didn't have to wait long. Suddenly, a shadow blocked the light coming into the treasure chest. The chest vibrated with the sound of pounding, the coins jingling under us.

WHAM. WHAM. WHAM.

## I Treasure Your Barf

"Oh man," said Gordon. "I'm sorry if I made too much noise."

"Shhhh," I said as quietly as I could.

But it was too late. The lid of the treasure chest was flung back, and I stared at . . .

"Shane!" said Gordon. "You scared the—"

"Let us in," Shane hissed. "Ben needs somewhere to cough, and those bird things aren't too far down the hallway."

Shane tossed a green-faced Ben into the treasure chest and then climbed in himself.

I brought the lid down as slowly as I could.

As soon as it closed, Nabila screeched, "*Habibi!* I thought I had lost you!"

She went in for a kiss . . .

"Ew," said Gordon.

. . . and Ben promptly coughed a mouthful of sand into her face.

Shane slapped his back and encouraged him.

"That's right, hack it up, Ben," he said.

The treasure chest shook with Ben's coughing.

"Well, if those squawkers are nearby, we're done for," I said.

Ben continued to hack and cough.

"We got a good look at them," said Shane. "I think they had bird heads."

"Servants of Horus," said Nabila.

We all looked at her with blank stares.

"Horus is an ancient Egyptian god of war who was connected to the pharaohs," she added. "If Murray has somehow taken control of his servants, Horus will not be pleased."

Ben continued hacking until it turned into gagging.

"Oh no," said Gordon. "I know that sound. He's gonna blow."

And blow Ben did. He let loose a sandy, stinky blast

of chunks all over us—and the treasure.

SCHHHWAAAAAAARF!

Gordon jumped up to push the heavy lid off the treasure chest.

Shane grabbed him and pulled him back down into the barfy gold.

"They were right behind us!" whispered Shane into Gordon's ear.

"I. Can't." Gordon gagged. "I can't hold. It. In. HUHWUUURRRRRP."

Gordon covered his mouth, but nothing came out.

"Just hold it in," said Nabila. "I thought you were the strong one."

"You don't even know what it smells like," said Gordon. "Lucky you."

"Trust me, I know how lucky I am," said Nabila. "But I also can't smell roses or fresh bread."

"I'm the lucky one," said Ben. "If you could smell, I don't think that we'd be dating."

"Oh man," said Gordon. "You said the D-word. Now I really am getting sick."

"Stop it," I said, but I shouldn't have opened my mouth.

All I could taste was Ben's barf. My eyes were getting watery from the smell. My stomach cramped up. Soon, Gordon wouldn't be the only one struggling to hold it in.

We all listened for the SQUAWK of the Servants of Horus.

"Well, I, for one, feel better," said Ben.

"Good for you," I said, a little drool dribbling from the side of my mouth. "Ugh. I think it's safe. Let's get out of here."

We rushed to get out of the chest, but with the treasure slippery from barf, it was tough.

Finally we all tumbled out, only to find Neferkare staring at us from the doorway. He was wrapping himself in fresh strips of cloth.

"Well," he said, "I suppose I did tell you to enjoy yourself with the treasure. I think you had a little too much fun."

He paused and eyed Nabila for a moment.

"You have no sense of smell, do you?" he asked her. "How else could you look so healthy after being locked in that vomit box?"

"It's true," she said. "Why do you ask?"

Before Neferkare could answer, Shane asked, "Can you lend us some of those rags to clean up?"

"Get your own," said Neferkare, and he kept walking. "Third door on the right down the hall," he said as he shuffled his way back toward the dungeon.

Gordon shook his head. "I don't think I like this *Nerfcare* guy."

"We're as clean as we're going to get without any water," said Ben as he examined a handful of filthy cloth wrappings. "If we had any water, I would have drunk it all anyway. I guess this is fine."

"Fine for you, Barf Breath," said Gordon. "We normal humans aren't used to having barf-covered clothes like you."

"We should hurry up," I said. "I don't want to stay in the same place for too long."

"Wait," said Nabila. "Give me a minute to explore this room. It contains the same weird hieroglyphs as Murray's ship."

"How's everything look, Shane?" I asked.

Shane was posted at the door. "All clear," he said.

"Okay," I said to Nabila. "But don't take *too* long."

"This room must be where mummification used to take place," she said.

"Creepy," said Ben.

"You've seen the wrappings," said Nabila, pointing to the now barf-soaked pile. She walked over to a shelf. "And these are canopic jars, where the different organs are placed before the mummification process begins."

"Cool," said Gordon. "Is Murray's heart in there? Maybe we could use it for ransom."

"You've forgotten that Murray doesn't have a heart," Ben said.

Nabila ignored the jokes and continued, "And this is a brain hook."

She held up a rusty-looking metal rod with a hook at the end.

"A brain what-now?" asked Gordon.

"This would be used to scramble the brains in the head and then pull them out of the body before it was mummified," Nabila responded.

"Ew," said Ben, looking green again.

"Oh, stop it," she said. "You've already blown enough chunks for one day—no more!"

She stared at the brain hook and looked lost for a moment.

"Nabila?" I asked. "Are you okay?"

She brought the hook up to her mouth, extended her tongue, and licked the very top of the hook.

"Uh . . . ," Gordon said.

Nabila flicked her tongue back into her mouth, and her eyes focused again.

"Sorry," she said. "After eating all those brains on the moon, I didn't think I'd ever want any more. But I sort of miss the flavor, you know?"

"Yeah, I do," said Shane, licking his teeth.

"Keep that in check!" Gordon said, and walked to the other side of the room.

"Did you get any?" asked Shane.

"Nope," Nabila said, and she shrugged. "Let's see if we can find a way out of this pyramid."

As we walked into the next room, I asked Nabila,

"Why didn't ancient Egyptians think the brain was important?"

"They didn't understand it as we do today," she replied. "They thought other parts of the body held the soul and mind—the stuff that made people do and say things."

"So why is Murray interested in the brain?" I asked. "Any ideas?"

"Not yet," said Nabila, "but I'm worried that a mummy as powerful as Neferkare would just give up so easily. We've always seen Murray as a conniving, grumpy old man—but it sounds like he has real power."

"You know about Neferkare?" I asked.

"I've read about him, yes," said Nabila. "He was one of the most powerful rulers in Egypt. He ruled for ninety-four years! And now he's napping in a chair for all eternity."

"Guys!" yelled Shane, his voice echoing down the hallway.

"Where's he going?" I hissed. "He's supposed to be on lookout!"

We rushed to the door, and down the hallway I could see Shane walking into another room.

"Guys," he called out. "Get in here right away!"

A boom echoed down the hallway, plaster shaking out of the bricks above our heads as we ran to our friend in the next room.

# King Toot

BOOM BOOM BOOM!

"Shane!" I yelled down the hallway. "Are you okay?"

"What's in there?" asked Gordon.

"This doesn't sound good," said Nabila.

We rushed into the room Shane had entered, and I was horrified!

BOOM BOOM BOOM!

"Shane," I hissed. "What are you doing?"

But I knew what Shane was doing. So did everyone else.

"Why are you banging that drum?" asked Nabila.

"Are you crazy?!" we all yelled at him.

Shane was standing on a platform in the back of the room in front of a huge drum. It looked like everything in the room was a musical instrument. Lutes. Flutes. Something that looked like a weird old recorder.

I ran over and snagged the stick Shane was holding out of his hand.

"What?" he asked. "Can't a guy have some fun? Murray's going to let us go as soon as he realizes he's being crazy. He's probably dancing to the music right now."

"I still think those creepy bird-heads might be wondering who's playing the giant drum," said Ben.

"Here," I said, grabbing a wooden recorder thing from a nearby table and shoving it into Shane's hand. "If you're going to play something, play this."

"Awesome," he said, and put the recorder up to his lips to blow.

FFFFFFFTTTTTTT!

No sound came out.

Shane looked at the ancient instrument strangely and then put it back to his mouth, this time blowing harder.

FFFFFFTTTTTTTTPLOP!

A huge black spider tumbled out of the bottom of the recorder and landed in the sand. It immediately jumped up and skittered toward the door.

"Sorry, man!" said Shane. He held up the recorder to look down the bore and made sure there was nothing else.

Then he put it up to his lips.

TOOT-TOOT *toot-toot-toot.*

*Tut-tut-tut-tut-tut-tut-tut.*

*Toot-toot-toot.*

"'Iron Man'?" asked Gordon. "Why 'Iron Man'?"

"Why not?" asked Shane, and he kept playing.

"Maybe the drum wasn't so bad," Nabila said.

"Well, this is a lot quieter," I said to Nabila, and then turned to Shane. "But it could be even more quiet!"

He got the hint and played softly.

But he kept playing.

*Toot-toot.*

He played as we walked down the hallway and looked into a game room.

*Toot-toot-toot.*

"That's the biggest Senet board I've ever seen," said Nabila.

"What's Senet?" asked Ben.

"It's an ancient Egyptian board game," said Nabila. "It was buried in tombs along with the mummies so they'd have something to play during their trip to the afterlife."

Shane stopped playing for a moment and said, "Wow. We've got music. We've got games. I don't want to die, but if I had to, this would be the perfect place."

"Stop talking like that," I said. "We're not going to die here. We just need to find a way out. Let's keep going. And give it a rest, would you?"

Making our way down the hallway, we passed small rooms filled with nothing more than an occasional chair or a small bit of treasure.

"Yawn," said Gordon after we opened the third massive treasure chest. "Forget gold. I could use a hamburger."

"Even a Blandburger," I said.

We kept walking and walking and walking down the hallway. After a while, the strange hieroglyphs we had seen on the spaceship appeared once again.

Nabila grabbed a torch from one of the holders along the wall and passed it over the hieroglyphs.

"Hmmm," she mumbled. "Sense of smell."

"What is it?" I asked, hopeful she had somehow deciphered a way to create a door out of thin air.

But she didn't say anything. The torch just crackled in her hand, and she had a funny look on her face.

"Nabila?" Ben asked, walking over to her. "Are you okay?"

"Yes," she said, snapping out of it. "I think what this is saying is that the person buried within this tomb had no sense of smell. Just like me. Strange, right?"

"Do we need to figure out what it means?" I asked.

"No, no, no!" she said. "Let's keep going."

"I'm so tired," said Gordon. "This gravity is killing me."

"You're right," said Ben. "I feel so weighed down. I got used to the moon."

"We just have to keep going," I said, even though I was tired and smelled like barf. I just wanted to be back home with all the old monsters—they had become my family over the last few months.

"I wonder where Director Z is," I said.

"Back home at Gallow Manor. Probably wondering where we are," said Shane.

"Do you think he tracked the ship?" I asked. "Do you think he knows that we're trapped in Egypt?"

Nobody answered.

We slowly walked down the hall for what seemed like forever and then went into another room.

It was filled with mummified cats. They were lined up in rows that seemed to go an insanely long distance into the back of the room.

"Weird," said Gordon. The room was cold and smelled funny.

"There must be hundreds of them!" I said. My voice echoed through the room.

"Egyptians were often buried with cats to keep

them happy in the afterlife," said Nabila.

"Everyone loves a pet," said Ben.

"Cool," said Shane, "a captive audience." He walked up to the first cat in the first row and began to TOOT-TOOT once again.

"Shane . . . why?" I said. "Come on, let's keep searching for a way out of here."

He stopped, and a low MEOOOOOOW echoed through the chamber.

"Okay," I said. "Now it's really starting to get weird."

HISSSSSSS!

"Uh, guys," said Gordon, pointing to the back of the room. "Look!"

A shadow stirred.

## Here, Kitty, Kitty, Kitty!

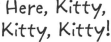

MEOOOOWWWHISSSS!

"What did you do, Shane?" I asked.

One of the mummified cats from waaaaaaaaay back in the room, the third row over, creakily walked over to Shane.

"Meeeooow?" it asked. Its neck bones cracked as it turned its head inquisitively.

"Awesome!" yelled Shane. He reached down to scratch its ears.

"Be careful, Shane!" said Ben.

But the cat was happy. It purred, and dust came out of its mouth.

"Leave it to Shane," said Ben. "He can make a new friend wherever he goes."

"I'm trying to remember where I read about the Thousand Mummified Cats," Nabila said. "There's only one tomb that has this many, and if we knew where we were, it might help us get out of here."

The cat stretched, cracking joints that hadn't been used in two or three millennia. It ran out of the room and into the hallway.

"Maybe we should follow it," said Shane. "Cats always seem to know where they're going."

We jumped into the hallway and followed the cat. It pawed its way past two rooms and then entered the third one. The room was small and completely empty, except for a golden sarcophagus propped up against the back wall.

The cat went over and meowed in front of the sarcophagus, pawing the foot of the massive gold figure.

"Maybe it's another mummy that could help us out of here," I said, and searched for a way to open the sarcophagus.

"Look," said Nabila.

She forced her fingers into a small seam and made it a little bit larger. Gordon stuck his beefy fingers in and grunted as he forced the sarcophagus open.

CREEEEEEEEEEAAAAAAAK!

The sarcophagus opened wide, and there was nothing in it.

"That's disappointing," said Shane. "I was hoping someone would pop out to greet us."

The mummified cat walked right into the sarcophagus and started pawing at the wall.

"What is it, Kitty?" asked Gordon.

Gordon walked up to the wall and pushed on it. There was the sound of gears grinding into place, and then the wall moved in and slid to the side, revealing . . .

"The music room," I yelled. "It's a shortcut. But we've got to keep looking for a way out of here!"

I shooed the cat out of the sarcophagus, and Gordon slammed it shut again.

"Meeeeeow?!" the cat said, staring at me through its wrappings.

"Show us how to get out of here," I said to the cat. "We don't want to go back the way we came. And we don't want to get close to any of those bird-heads."

The cat looked like it shrugged a *whatever*, and then it padded over to Shane. Shane picked it up and stroked it while it purred.

"Are you okay, little guy?" Shane cooed. "Should I take off your wrappings and free you up a little bit?"

Shane began to unravel the cat's mummy wrappings,

but the cat hissed and swatted at him. He tried to put the cat down, but it swatted at him again. He lifted it up and cradled it.

"Okay, fine," Shane said.

"Let's keep moving," I said.

We headed down the hallway, away from the Room of One Thousand Mummified Cats.

We passed more treasure and more treasure and *more*.

"Enough with the gold," I said. "I want a door out of here."

"I don't even know how we got here," said Nabila. "I'm just so tired that I got turned around."

"Well, now we have that shortcut," said Shane. "Thanks, Kitty!"

The cat was asleep in Shane's arms. It must have been exhausting standing still for a few thousand years.

"That's not fair," said Ben. "Aside from the brief little concussion-induced nap I took when I first got here, I haven't slept at all since we left for the moon."

We finally reached the end of the hallway, and there was only one room left.

"Man, I really hope that there's a door on the other side of that room," I said.

We ducked inside to find nothing.

"Of course," I said, slumping down, exhausted. "We must have passed seven other hallways on the way here.

We'll have to head back and explore those."

"Can't we take a break first?" asked Ben. "I literally can't think. I mean I think I can't think. I just don't know what I think."

"Yeah, it would probably be a good idea," I said. "We're not going to get out of here if we can't even think straight."

This room, like all of the others, was just a single room, built into the blocks, with a sand floor. There didn't seem to be anything in it, but there were a few of those weird hieroglyphs again.

"What do those mean?" I asked Nabila.

"I have no idea," she said. "But I see a lot of symbols for what I *think* is *scorpion*."

"Scorpion?" I asked, yawning. "Let's go to sleep. We can figure this out after a little nap."

"What?!" she said. "We can't all go to sleep. I'll stand guard for a half hour. And while I do, I'll start working on these hieroglyphs."

I wanted to say "Thanks," but I fell asleep before I could.

# A Serpo-WHAT?!

I don't know how long it was before an earthquake woke me up.

"Hurry," I mumbled. "Run. Earthquake. The pyramid will collapse."

"It's not an earthquake, and we don't know if we're actually in a pyramid," said Nabila, shaking me. "It's me. Wake up!"

"What it is?" I said. "Me so tired."

"The hieroglyphs!" yelled Nabila.

"We have to get out of here. Help me wake up the others!"

"Wait," I said. "Why? What's going on?!"

Nabila ran over to Ben. "Wake up, *habibi*!"

I ran to Shane and slapped his cheeks. He jumped up, and the mummified cat flew off of his chest, hitting the sand with a choked "MEW."

"Get up," I said.

"What's going on?" he asked.

"I have no idea!" I said. "Get Gordon up."

I ran back over to Nabila, who was helping Ben.

"Why are we rushing?" I asked. "You have to tell me."

Suddenly, the sand in the back of the room started to shift. It flowed forward, and something appeared to be moving under the shifting sand.

"More scarabs?" asked Gordon groggily.

Then I could see them—behind each was a stinger, pointing in the air.

"Scorpions," Nabila said.

"Even better," said Gordon. "Bring 'em on!"

"According to the hieroglyphs, the scorpions are a curse for anyone who stays longer than a half hour in this room," said Nabila. "They won't sting you anywhere but in the eye."

"Yay!" said Shane, grabbing his recorder. "I was really hoping that they wouldn't be ankle-stingers."

Soon the room had filled with giant scorpions.

"We've got to go!" I yelled. "We can lose them at the shortcut."

The mummified cat shook the sand out of its wrappings and darted for the door. I don't speak cat, but the way it meowed at me, I could have sworn that it said, "I told you so."

Now the room really was shaking as more and more scorpions spewed up into the room. They moved forward, tumbling over one another as they came.

"Go!" I yelled.

We burst out of the room and down the hall. The cat was already long gone. Nabila ran side-by-side with me.

"They're right behind us," Shane said. "Keep moving."

We rounded a corner, and I looked back to see Gordon, Ben, Shane . . . and a wall of scorpions flowing down the hallway

I looked ahead and ran even harder now, my shoes sinking into the sand as I pushed forward as fast as I could.

"It's just ahead," I shouted. "Gordon, get ready to open that sarcophagus."

"How are we going to close it?" asked Nabila.

"I have no idea," I said. "But I don't know what else to do. We've just got to take our chances."

We turned into the room to see Shane's new friend,

the mummified cat, hissing at the sarcophagus.

"Out of the way, Kitty!" I yelled.

The cat held its ground.

Gordon rushed past it and began to open the sarcophagus as the rest of our friends poured into the room, followed by a tidal wave of scorpions.

"Cover your eyes!" yelled Nabila. "They'll only sting your eyes!"

I did what Nabila told us. The wave of scorpions knocked me over and covered me head to toe. I could hear them click against each other as they crawled around. I could feel their pincers probe my hands, but I wasn't about to drop them from my eyes.

"Gordon, get that thing open!" yelled Ben. "We have to—BLECK!"

"Ben?" yelled Shane.

"I think a scorpion got in my mouth!" he replied. "I'm okay."

They crawled all over me. It was driving me crazy. Eventually, they started to pinch my hands, trying to get me to expose my eyes. My hands burned, but I wouldn't give in.

And then all of a sudden, WHOOOOOSH, the scorpions dropped to the ground and ran toward the door.

"Aw, yeah!" I said.

Then I looked up at the open sarcophagus.

"Uhh, guys?" Gordon said. He stepped back slowly.

A huge creature with the body of a leopard and the head of a cobra walked through the sarcophagus.

"A serpopard!" said Nabila.

"A what now?" asked Gordon.

"It's part serpent and part leopard," she replied.

Gordon just looked at her. "So . . . should I freeze? Should I run? Nabila?"

"I don't remember seeing it before," said Shane.

"RUN!" yelled Ben.

We ran with the scorpions through the doorway and turned to the right.

Behind us, a great HISSROAR filled the hallway as the serpopard ran down the passage.

"Okay," said Ben. "I'm ready to go back to my prison now."

"Which way is back?!" I yelled.

"Turn right," said Nabila.

HISSROAR!

The serpopard reared its huge, snaky head and lunged at Gordon. It missed and bit off a chunk of rock instead. We turned a corner while it chomped on its snack.

"In here," I yelled, ducking into a room. "Maybe we can block the entrance."

As soon as I entered the room, I knew it was a

bad idea. It smelled terrible—like the muckiest swamp water with the deadest fish.

All around me were buckets of chunky, gooey liquid.

I held my T-shirt up to my nose and looked around for something to block the door.

"Over there!" I yelled to my friends. "That long metal table. Let's get it up on its side and cover the door!"

All of us tipped it over and moved it into place, and BANG. The serpopard burst through, knocking us down. I landed on my butt and slid all the way back to a trash can filled with murky water and something floating at the top that look a lot like a brain. A little of the dirty water splashed over the side and onto my face.

"Blech!" I yelled, and wiped off my face, careful to keep it out of my eyes.

"Chris!" Ben yelled. I opened my eyes—and was face-to-face with the serpopard!

It opened its serpent mouth and struck, grabbing me by the neck.

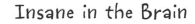

## Insane in the Brain

"HRRRRRLLLP!" I yelled, choked by powerful serpopard jaws.

"Chris!" I could hear Shane scream as I started to pass out. "Hold on!"

And then that annoying sound filled the air.

TOOT-TOOT *toot-toot-toot.*

The serpopard let me go, and I fell with a splash into the huge brain tank it had backed up next to.

At first, I was too stunned to breathe.

*Tut-tut-tut-tut-tut-tut-tut.*

*Why can't Shane stop playing "Iron Man"?* I wondered, floating in a sea of brains. It was so relaxing, so—

Then, suddenly, I realized I would die if I didn't breathe. I gasped without thinking and sucked in disgusting brain juice and gray particles. I flailed and choked and made my way to the surface of the tank.

"Aaaaah!" I screeched, finally breathing. "Get me out of here!"

I collapsed over the side of the tank, and Gordon helped me out. I flopped on the floor like a fish. My body felt so weird. I rolled over to try to get up and saw that the serpopard had fallen deeply asleep. Shane stroked the hairy ears on its scaly head.

"Shane's recorder playing put it to sleep," said Nabila. "I can't believe it. I thought that you were going to die!"

"I still feel like I'm going to," I croaked. "I think I ate brains. I totally drank some of the brain juice."

My stomach clenched, and my vision got blurry.

"Chris, are you okay?" asked Ben.

I couldn't answer him—I put my head back on the cold, dirty ground and gritted my teeth to keep from passing out.

I took in one breath, opened my eyes . . .

. . . and saw the ceiling of a vaguely familiar room.

"Um, guys?" I asked. My voice no longer echoed. The room smelled like musk instead of mold and ancient earth.

I looked down to see my insanely hairy body covered by a sheet.

"What?!" I growled in a voice that was not my own.

I lifted myself off the bed. It was difficult, because, on top of being hairy, I was huge.

I jumped onto the floor with a THUD. A few coins rolled off the top of a dresser. Some fell into an open sock drawer, and others rolled noisily on the polished hardwood floor. I looked down to see a few of them roll into my feet—which were just as hairy as the rest of my body.

I looked up to see a full-length mirror swaying back and forth, still in motion from the great THUD. I walked over and held it in place with one huge hairy paw.

I looked into the mirror, and my mouth fell wide open.

Well, not my mouth.

ROY's mouth. I was the Bigfoot, and I was back at Gallow Manor.

Suddenly, the door was flung open, and Director Z stuck his head into the room.

"Roy," his voice boomed, "how many times have I told you that you need to exit your bed slowly?"

I turned to Director Z and tried to say "It's me, Chris!" but all that came out was, "ARRRRGGGBBBBLLLRRGGGG!" as I rushed toward him.

"Roy, wait!" said Director Z. "Calm yourself!"

"I'm not Roy," I was finally able to yell as Director Z disappeared. "I'm Chris!"

"Was there ever any doubt?" asked Shane.

"Shane?" I asked.

I turned around to see my friends staring at me. The serpopard continued to sleep peacefully.

"I've come back," I said, feeling slightly nauseated. I reached up to my nose, which was running.

"Where were you going?" asked Gordon. "To puke up some brains? You shot right up and started running!"

"I was running toward Director Z," I said. Now snot was pouring out of my nose.

"What do you mean?" asked Ben. "You saw him?"

Ben jumped up from the dusty rock he was sitting on and rushed to the entrance, looking for Director Z.

"No," I called to Ben, flinging snot accidentally as I reached out my hand to grab him. "I was back at Gallow Manor. I was in Roy's body! And I saw Director Z!"

"Yo, what is coming out of your nose?" asked Shane.

"Just snot," I said, holding up my fingers.

I nearly screamed when I saw what they were coated in.

"Gray matter?" I asked in disbelief. "My brains?!"

"Did someone say 'brains'?" Nabila asked, and she zoomed over to me so fast, I swear she left a trail of dust in her wake. The next thing I knew, she was noisily slurping the gray matter off of my fingers. Ben got a nervous look on his face.

"This is the most disgusting thing I've ever seen in my life," Gordon said. "Stop her, Chris!"

"No way, dude!" I yelled. "I gotta know if that gray stuff is my brains."

"Mmmm," she started to say, but then she spat onto the ground in disgust.

"What is it?" I asked, worried. "Are my brains ruined forever?"

"BLECK," she said, trying not to gag. "Those are definitely brains, but they're not yours. They taste ancient."

"Ancient *Egyptian*?" asked Shane. "Is it the brain snack he just had? Is that what's oozing out of him?"

Before Nabila could answer, an angry grumble echoed down the hallway.

"Murrayhotep!" Ben whispered in panic, and ran from the doorway.

"We've got to hide," I whispered.

"Behind the brain tank!" said Gordon, and he ducked behind it. We followed quickly, and in the rush, Ben kicked up a huge cloud of dust. I gulped in a mouthful and let out a massive, brain-splattered sneeze.

"Chris!" Nabila hissed once we were crouched down behind the tank. "I'm sure he heard you!"

She grabbed my arm and held on tightly, as if her squeeze would keep the big bad mummy from seeing us. There were two or three inches of space between the tank and the floor, so I lay down on the ground to peek into the room.

Murrayhotep shuffled through the door. His bandaged feet stopped in front of the tank.

It was eerily silent.

"What was that noise?" he grumbled.

His feet shuffled over to the right side of the tank, and I knew that he was about to peek behind it . . .

## The Mummy Returns

Murrayhotep had slowly made his way around the brain tank, when . . .

BLLLAA-CHOOO!

But it wasn't me that sneezed this time. It was the serpopard.

Murrayhotep shuffled over to the serpopard. Nabila finally loosened her grip, and we all looked at each other like *whew!*

"Get up, you overgrown lazy cat!"

Murrayhotep said. "There's no sleeping on the job when I'm around!"

I pushed my head right into the cold sand so I could see what was happening.

Murrayhotep lifted one ragged, dusty foot and kicked the serpopard in the stomach, hard.

But it just made the serpopard snore.

"Why do I feed you all the Nile rats your lazy heart desires if you're just going to fall asleep guarding the most important room in my entire pyramid?"

He kicked the serpopard again, harder this time, but the huge beast just grunted.

"I'll deal with you later," Murrayhotep said. "I've got bigger fish to fry, and not much time to fry them."

He began walking around the room, chanting in front of each container as he went along.

". . . ANUBIS-DUN-MAR-HOTEP-RA . . ."

"What's he saying?" I whispered in Nabila's ear.

"It's a blessing of some sort," she said. "I think it has to do with herbal potions. He's chanting to the gods to thank them for the herbs that will transform his minds."

"Minds?" I asked. "As in plural?"

She held her finger up to her mouth as Murrayhotep once again stepped in front of the tank we were hiding behind.

"You're my biggest batch, so I've saved most of the herbs for you," he said. "Now, stew, my brains, stew.

Soon it will be time to put our plan in motion."

The jars, garbage pails, and tanks of brains vibrated, spilling more juices. A huge glop of black goo dropped onto Gordon's head.

Gordon reached up to his head and was about to yell, but Shane covered his mouth fast. A glop of black hit Shane's hand just as he did so.

"Don't worry," Murrayhotep said soothingly to his brains. "You have a little more time to stew. There are five more brains I'll be adding to my collection. Young, strong brains."

The brains stopped jiggling in their containers, but now my friends and I shook with fear.

*Murrayhotep wants to pickle our brains,* I thought. My brain didn't want to be pickled.

Now Ben gripped my arm tightly. I had to clench my jaw to keep from saying "Ow!"

"Speaking of our new brains," Murrayhotep continued, speaking to his captive audience, "I should probably go visit our guests. They need food! They need sweet nectar to drink! I can't have unhealthy brains spoiling our wonderful mix. It will take a few days to make them strong again after the brutal crash landing I subjected them to, but then we'll harvest their wonderful brains! Then it's time! Our time!"

Murrayhotep left the room, and I immediately jumped up.

"We can't let Murrayhotep know we escaped," I said. "We've got to get back to the prison."

"You mean we have to swim through sand again?" said Ben, looking green.

"Yes, we've got to," I said. "Let's go to the sarcophagus shortcut and get back in there before him. Otherwise he'll know that we're free, and he's *not* going to be happy about it!"

I poked my head into the torch-filled hallway. As soon as I saw Murrayhotep go around the next corner, I waved to my friends, and we ran out as quietly as we could.

We ran down to the corner, waited until Murrayhotep was out of sight, and hustled into the room with the sarcophagus.

The golden sarcophagus was still wide open, and we ran inside.

"Hurry, Gordon!" I yelled.

Gordon pushed the wall like he had before, and it slid open to reveal the music room.

"We should close it if we can," I said. "So we don't give away that we've been wandering around."

Gordon pointed to a lever on the wall and shrugged.

"Well, push it back into place!" I said. "Hurry!"

Gordon shoved the lever up, hard, and there was a click from within the stonework. The wall began to slide back into place as the sarcophagus closed from the other side.

"All right, let's go!" said Nabila.

"Meow!"

"Kitty!" yelled Shane, pointing past the closing wall.

"It'll be fine," I said. "Leave it!"

But Shane walked over to the sliding wall and held it in place.

GRRRRRRRRRRRRRPPPPP!

Gears ground to a halt somewhere behind the wall.

"Don't break it—we might need it later," Ben said.

The mummified cat ran into the room, and Shane let the wall go.

With a BOOM it slammed into place.

"Let's hope Murrayhotep didn't hear that," I said.

We ran back down the hallway toward the pile of sand we had crawled out of before.

"Remember, don't breathe in the sand, and keep pushing!" I said.

Shane dove in, followed by the mummified cat, then Gordon, Nabila, and Ben.

Once Ben's wiggling shoes disappeared under the sand, I took a huge breath and followed.

*Push, push, push, hold it, push, push.*

It wasn't any better than the time before. Stars danced in front of my closed eyes again, but this time I didn't panic. I felt Ben in front of me and grabbed on to his shoes.

SSCHLOOOOOOOP!

Someone had pulled out Ben, and then I came out.

But I couldn't tell who had pulled us out: It was dark again, pitch-black.

Ben was coughing, but I felt great as I took in a huge breath.

To our right, a stone slowly scraped out of place. A ray of light brightened up the room.

"Get away from the sand tunnel," I whispered. "And act sick, no matter what. We want Murray to think we're sick and not ready to have our brains removed."

Ben gave a thumbs-up and kept coughing.

I concentrated to change my face from happy that I had made it through the sand tunnel without choking to sad and sick.

"Uuuuuugh!" I moaned as Murrayhotep walked into the room.

He was followed by the two Servants of Horus.

We all did our best acting, rolling and moaning on the floor.

"My deepest apologies," said Murrayhotep. "I never meant to leave you children in here so long, and I—"

Murrayhotep stared behind us. I rolled over, moaning, to see what he was looking at.

The mummified cat sat between Shane and Nabila.

"What is that cat doing here?" Murrayhotep growled.

# So Hungry

"'That cat'?" I asked. "What cat?"

I realized that I sounded healthy, so I added an "Uuugh!"

"Meow," said the mummified cat.

"No creature should be able to get into this room," growled Murrayhotep. "It makes me think that you could all get out." He eyed every corner of the room suspiciously. "Have you been exploring?"

My friends, panicked, suddenly quieted down to whispers.

When Murray's back was turned, I motioned to them to keep moaning.

"Soooooo siiiiiiiick," said Gordon as he rolled and clutched his stomach.

"Nooooooo," said Nabila.

Murray's gaze moved slowly over the pile of sand we had burst through to get back into the room, but before he could say anything—

"That dusty old thing?" said Neferkare, rising slowly from his chair. "Why, that was my sole companion in this room before these children got here. Kitty! Come here, cat!"

The cat cocked its head, confused, but still ran over to Neferkare and jumped up into his arms. Neferkare sat down and patted the cat's head. Small clouds of dust puffed off the cat.

"It might have been two millennia ago," said Murrayhotep, "but I distinctly remember burying you with nothing but the chair you're currently rotting in."

"This cat was secretly within my wrappings," said Neferkare. "Soon after I was imprisoned here, I unwrapped myself to pull it out, and then wrapped myself up again."

Murrayhotep stared at Neferkare for what seemed like forever. I was still rolling around on the ground, moaning, but I looked up at Murrayhotep and wasn't sure if he believed Neferkare's lie.

Murrayhotep's face lit up, and he laughed. "Ah-huh-huh-huh-haaaaa! I always thought your butt was too big for a hundred-year-old. That must be where you hid it! You dusty old fart!"

Murrayhotep sighed and turned back to us. Through my squinting eyes I could see he looked extremely concerned.

*Our act is working,* I thought.

I clenched my jaw and let out my best "Uuuuuuugh" up to that point.

"Tsk-tsk," said Murrayhotep. "Perhaps I was too hard on you after all. My apologics, children, but I have just the thing to help make you feel better."

He clapped his hands twice, and the Servants of Horus left the room.

"What?" gasped Gordon, writhing on the floor. "Are they going to cut off our heads? Please let them cut our heads off."

"Oh, no, no, no," said Murrayhotep, walking over to Gordon and helping him sit up. "My servants are fetching you a feast, and when you're done feasting, I'll cover you in herb-infused oils that will help your minds . . . uh, relax."

"Just kill us," said Nabila. "Our heads ache so much. I can't think."

Ben, Shane, and I all moaned, "Yessssss."

"Strange," said Murrayhotep. "I thought my protection charm would have kept you from harm during the crash . . . The ship was fine . . ."

Murrayhotep scratched his chin, but before he could think too deeply, the Servants of Horus came back into the room. Though they had bird heads, their bodies were muscular and strong, and each carried a massive table, carefully balancing it so the silver dishes on top didn't slide off.

"Well, hurry it up, then!" yelled Murray. "Can't you see these children are in need of food?"

SQUAWK! SQUAWK!

They put the tables down.

"I've had only the finest cuisine prepared for you," said Murray. "Macaroni and cheese!"

A bird-head lifted up a silver lid to reveal a steaming pile of liquid gold.

"Cheeseburgers, cooked perfectly!" announced Murray.

Another cover was lifted, and the smell of delicious hamburger filled the room.

"The buns are perfect," said Shane. "Where did you get such perfect buns, Murray?"

"I have my ways," said Murray. "We have fried chicken, hot dogs, perfectly cooked spaghetti and meatballs . . ."

The bird-heads kept lifting silver lids and revealed an amazing amount of food. My stomach grumbled with delight. I had barely eaten anything since we left for the moon a few days before.

Gordon stepped up to the table and grabbed a fried chicken leg. His eyes were wild, and he was smiling.

"See," said Murrayhotep. "You'll feel better as soon as you've eaten. I'll leave you to your meal. Enjoy." He turned to go.

Before Gordon could chomp on the juicy, savory chicken, Ben snatched it out of his hand.

"Wait," said Ben. "Let me go first. I'm weaker and scrawnier than you."

"There's enough for everyone," said Murray, turning back.

But Ben dug into the chicken and then pushed Gordon back into the sand.

"MMMM," said Ben. He chewed wildly and drooled.

Murray bent down to help Gordon back up. When he did, Ben gave the other three of us a look like *watch me.*

"MMMM," said Ben again. "MMMMMMMMARF!"

And he threw up all over Gordon and Murray.

"My wrappings!" yelled Murray, and he tried desperately to scrape off the barely digested chicken chunks.

WHAAAAAARF!

Again, Ben spewed all over Murray.

Nabila, Shane, and I looked at each other with disgust, knowing what we had to do, and approached the table.

I grabbed a spoonful of macaroni and cheese, the Servants of Horus nodding in approval.

BLLLLLLLLLLLLLARF!

I threw up all over their bird heads.

SPLLLLLLUUUUUUURF!

Shane threw up all over Nabila.

WHHHHHHHHAAAAAARFFFFUH!

Nabila threw up right into Gordon's mouth.

BLLLLLURCH!

Gordon spewed Nabila's spew into Murray's face and fell over on the ground twitching.

"How are your brains going to stay healthy if you're throwing up your food?" yelled Murray, covered in stomach juice.

"Brains?" I asked, drooling a stream of barf. "What do you mean by that?"

I wiped a few chunks away from my mouth for effect.

"Servants!" yelled Murray. "Gather up the tables and let's leave these children to stew in their filth!"

The servants and Murray ran out of the room, and the wall scraped back into place with a THUD.

"Ah-hah-hah-hah-haaaaaaah!" Neferkare laughed.

"I wish I had enough juices left to barf. That was stupendous!"

"That was torture," said Nabila.

"At least you barfed your own barf," said Gordon. He retched again.

"At least they left some torches in the room," I said.

"At least I snagged these when they weren't looking," said Shane, and he held up a jug of water and the juiciest, largest, most amazing hamburger in the history of ancient Egyptian hamburgers.

"Can Murray hear us through the prison walls?" I asked Neferkare.

"No," said Neferkare.

"YAAAAAHOOOOO!" I yelled.

## I Feel Like a Zombie

Shane leaned back and picked his teeth with a piece of the box we had shattered to make the fire.

"Thanks, everyone, for letting me have the biggest chunk of hamburger," he said. "It made me forget that I'm covered in barf for the second time today."

"You deserved the lion's share. You were the one who snagged the burger for us," said Gordon. "My piece changed my life. Now if I could just sleep for twenty-four hours."

"It was bad enough that you woke me up from a millennial slumber," said Neferkare from his seat. "Don't go making me hungry. The only thing to eat around here is this mummified cat."

The cat screeched and jumped off of Neferkare's lap. It padded over to Shane and jumped into his arms.

"It's okay, Kitty," said Shane. "He didn't mean it."

"We should probably think of another name for Kitty," said Gordon.

"Cleopatra?" asked Ben.

"Not original enough," replied Shane. "This little girl's one in a million."

"How do we know it's a girl?" asked Gordon. "And there weren't a million cats in that chamber, by the way."

"We shouldn't be thinking about Kitty's name right now," I said. "Did you guys forget there's a maniacal mummy waiting outside of this prison to fatten us up and take out our brains? Think about *that*, because we might not have long to think."

"Chris is right," said Nabila. "You were wrong, Shane. Murray's not going to let us go."

"That remains to be seen," he said.

"We need to move fast," I said. "We've got to get back to the pickled brains and . . ."

I gagged, and a little hamburger came back up into my mouth with leftover brains. I swallowed both.

"And what?" asked Gordon.

"I've got to eat some more brains and hope they take me back to Gallow Manor," I said. "We've spent the last few months saving those crazy old monsters. Now it's their turn to help us."

"Perfect timing," said Ben. "They're finally strong enough."

"So, I need to let them know we're in Egypt," I said. "We're lucky that all I have to do is eat a spoonful of brains, but I'm just not looking forward to it."

"Why don't I do it for you?" asked Shane. "Save you the trip."

"No," I said. "I'm worried I'm only able to do it because I have the pendant."

"Oh . . . ," said Shane. "I get it. It might connect you to the monsters somehow."

"Pendant?" said Nabila. "What pendant? What did I miss?"

"Since we left for the moon, I've had a pendant," I said. "I'm a Director."

"Wow," said Ben. "Congrats. That's awesome. Where is it?"

"I ate it," I said. "It's somewhere in my intestines."

"Whoa!" said Gordon. "You ate it? How'd you hold it in for so long?"

"I didn't," I said. "I ate it a second time on the moon."

"You mean after you . . . ," Gordon started to say.

All of my friends took a second to think about that.

"Thanks," said Neferkare. "Now I'm not so hungry."

"Anyway," I said, "that's why I think I've got to be the one to eat the brains. But I need you guys to help me get back there."

"The Chamber of Pickled Brains," said Shane. "Let's do it! I, for one, could use a little sand swim after my meal."

Without saying another word, he dove headfirst into the sand tunnel.

"Let's go," I said.

"Good luck," said Neferkare. "Tell all the pharaohs I say hello!"

There was no sign of the crazy bird-heads or Murray as we quietly made our way to the Chamber of Pickled Brains.

But when we neared the room, we could see that the serpopard was no longer napping.

"It's just pacing around in there," I said. "Shane, play it another tune."

"I left my recorder in the prison," said Shane.

"You what?!" I hissed.

"It's okay. I don't need it anymore," he said. "I'll handle this! It's not like it's Ammit the Devourer."

Shane walked boldly into the room.

"Shane!" yelled Nabila. "Stop!"

We all grabbed at him, but he was too fast.

"Hi there!" Shane said to the serpopard. "How was your nap?"

The serpopard turned to Shane and lowered its head to face him. It hissed and arched its back. The cat hair on its snake head stood up straight.

Shane didn't back down.

"I know you've got a pretty bad stomachache," said Shane. "But that's not our fault. In fact, if you leave this room right now, we're going to make a braincall to some friends who will talk some sense into Murray. And then I don't think he'll be kicking you in your stomach anymore."

The serpopard sat down and made a MEOW-HISS sound.

Shane reached up to scratch the beast's ear.

"I can't watch," said Ben, and he turned away.

"That's a good serpopard," said Shane.

PURRRRRRRRR.

"Now why don't you go off and guard another part of the pyramid," Shane said. "We've got some business to take care of in here. That braincall, remember?"

In a flash, the giant cat-serpent jumped up on all fours and zoomed out of the room, blowing sandy air in our faces as it ran down the hall.

"Come on," I said. "Let's get in there before it changes its mind."

The smell of the room made my stomach cramp.

"I'd better just do this, or I'm going to throw up all over myself," I said.

"This one doesn't smell as much," said Shane, holding up a mason jar.

He brought it over to me, and I peeked inside.

The brain quivered.

Ben gagged.

"You're not helping," I said.

I reached in and pinched off a piece of it.

Black-blue gunk oozed out of the wound, and the brain quivered even more.

"Sorry," I said. "I had to."

I popped the piece into my mouth.

MUNCH MUNCH MUNCH!

"Can you still see us?" said Shane. "Am I turning into Director Z?"

My vision got blurry, and my stomach cramped double-time. I felt absolutely terrible. I bent over to clutch my stomach, and when I was able to handle the pain, I looked back up . . .

. . . to see that I was in the forest behind Gallow Manor.

It was dark and hard to see anything, but I could hear muffled voices.

". . . where Murray first took off from . . . help determine where the children might be . . . search the crater for clues . . ."

It was so hard to think. I felt like my brain was in a blender. I was in pain from head to toe, and so hungry. I looked down at my hands and saw that chunks of flesh were peeling off.

*Zombie*, I thought. *I need to talk. How?*

A few of the zombies talked, but only after years of speech therapy. I stood there desperately trying to form words in my head, but it was hard. I felt absolutely rotten.

A tall figure grabbed my shoulder.

"John!" it yelled, terrifying me. "Why did you wander away? We've got a lot of work to do."

*Frederick!* His huge bulk was pieced together from dead flesh and brought to life with electricity. He looked young and fresh, just like the other monsters when the moon gave them their powers back.

*You look great*, I wanted to say.

"Ugh!" is all I said.

"No excuses," said Frederick. "We've all got to pitch in to find the kids."

Frederick dragged me to the edge of the crater that had been created when Murrayhotep's ship took off for the moon. Director Z crouched down in the very center, examining the burned chunks of tree and rock for clues.

"Uuugh!" I yelled at Director Z.

He looked up and said, "Ah, good. Frederick and John, start at the westernmost edge of the crater and make your way down, looking for anything out of the ordinary. A shard of metal. Charred zombie parts. Anything that wouldn't normally be found in the forest."

Words suddenly started forming in my mind. My head was clearing. The brain ooze was wearing off.

I had to act quickly.

I kicked Frederick's ankle, and his grip loosened.

"OWWW," yelled Frederick. Electricity sparked off of his head. "Why did you do that?"

I flung myself down into the crater before he could say anything else. I rolled fast, hitting rocks and stumps, and banging poor John's body. I could feel my mind quickly leaving John as I came to a stop at Director Z's feet.

"EGYPT!" I screeched as loudly as I could. "WE'RE IN EGYPT! HELP US! IT'S ME! IT'S—"

"Chris, are you okay?" asked Nabila.

I blinked and saw my friends where Director Z had been. Instead of trees, I was looking at the sandy ceiling of a room I didn't recognize.

"Where am I?" I asked.

"You rolled out of the room, down the hall, and into this little room," Ben said.

"And you were screaming!" said Nabila.

SQUAWK! SQUAWK! SQUAWK!

Gordon and Shane ducked into the room.

"They're coming down the hall," said Gordon.

"We've got to get to the shortcut and back to the prison cell, or we're caught for sure!"

"Can you do it?" asked Shane, helping me up.

"I'll try," I said. "I feel so weird, but let's go."

"Wait," said Nabila, pointing at my ear.

I reached up and felt something oozing down the side of my face.

Shane leaned in for a closer look.

"Leftover mummy brains," he said.

I scooped off a fingerful and looked at it.

"I'm really hoping none of this is my brains," I said.

SQUAWK!

"We gotta go!" yelled Gordon, and we rushed out of the room and down the hall.

## Brainstorm

"How'd you make it through the sand tunnel?" asked Gordon.

"I'm not sure," I said. "I can't really remember. I guess it's just second nature now."

"Do you feel better?" asked Shane.

"So much better," I said. "The next time you're tired, don't ever say you feel like a zombie. You don't even want to know how it feels to be a zombie."

"Oh, I know," said Nabila. "Even with the monster juice coursing through my veins, it felt pretty funky."

"Yeah, funky is actually the best way to describe it," I said. "I hope it was worth it. I hope that Director Z got the message. They might have just thought John went crazy."

"Maybe you should eat more brain?" asked Shane.

The hidden door started to scrape open again.

"They're coming in to investigate," I said. "Remember, we're totally tired. We're exhausted and sick."

"That's not going to be hard to pretend," said Gordon. "I think I'm getting a sore on my face."

"No, it's probably just a zit," replied Shane.

"My beautiful skin!" moaned Gordon.

"That's good, just like that," I said.

Murray stormed into the room.

"Why are you waking us up?" I squealed weakly. "We need rest. My head aches."

Murray looked around to see all of us in the room.

"If it wasn't you screaming, who was it?" Murray said.

We didn't answer.

He clapped his hands, and the Servants of Horus came in with a smaller set of tables. One was covered in breads, and the other had a number of metal flasks.

"I'm very sorry to disturb your slumber," said

Murrayhotep, walking around and patting each of us on the head. "Please, sleep. I've also brought you some much simpler food. Breads and juices. Perhaps I got carried away before."

"Can't eat," said Nabila. "Ugh." She drooled a little.

Murray walked over to Nabila and squeezed her drooly cheek.

"But, my dear," he said, "if you don't eat, then the crocodiles will."

Nabila swallowed hard.

"Now as much fun as that would be for me to watch," said Murrayhotep, "especially you, you spell-spewing snot, I just don't have the patience for that. Please don't waste my time."

Murrayhotep turned to the rest of us.

"Time!" he said. "I can't stay at my physical peak much longer, which means there's not much time for you to eat and regain your strength before I . . ."

Murrayhotep hesitated.

"Before you what?!" I choked out.

"No matter," he said. "There's no time to explain. Things are happening quite fast. I will give you one more day of rest, and then I'll need your . . . help."

"We'll never help you," said Gordon.

"My, you suddenly don't sound so tired, after all," said Murray.

I wanted to smack Gordon in the head for sassing

Murray. But before Gordon could answer, a scarab beetle shot out of the sand tunnel and scurried out the door.

Murray watched it go.

*Now he knows our secret,* I thought. *We're done for!*

"Wait!" yelled Murray to the scarab. "Don't go!"

He ran into the hall, and as the Servants of Horus closed the massive stone door, we could hear him yell, "The fastest ones are always the juiciest!"

"You should have kept your trap shut," I said to Gordon as soon as the door was closed.

"We need to stand up to him," said Gordon. "I've got basketball practice. We can't just sit and rot in this room for all eternity."

"Don't knock it until you've tried it," said Neferkare from his chair.

"Gordon's right," said Nabila. "If Murray sticks to his word, we have twenty-four hours before he'll be back. Our act worked, despite Gordon's mistake—"

"Hey!" yelled Gordon.

"—and now we need to capitalize on that," Nabila continued. "We can't just wait around in here. I need to figure out where we are so that the next time Chris eats brains, he can tell Director Z and the monsters."

I vurped a little brain into my mouth, but knew Nabila was right.

"Well, where's the safest room?" I asked Neferkare. "One where we might be able to make a stand."

"The one we're in is the safest room, if you ask me," he replied.

"Okay," I said, frustrated, "besides this room."

"I have no idea," he grumbled. "I've told you before, I don't even know where we are. That dried-up old feline probably has a better idea."

He pointed at Kitty, who was licking its paw in the darkest corner of the prison.

"*Pssst*," said Shane. "Here, Kitty!"

The cat came over, and Shane crouched down next to it.

"Can you take us to the safest place in this pyramid?" asked Shane.

The cat meowed and ran to the sand tunnel, its little cat butt wiggling in the air as it pushed into the sand.

"WAIT!" I yelled. "We have to gather up some food!"

We rushed to the tables and stuffed bread into our pockets. Each of us grabbed a huge flask of juice and greedily drank it down.

"Tastes so good!" I yelled, and dove into the sand.

By now, it had gotten quite easy to make it to the other side without running out of breath. I popped my head out of the sand to see the cat making its way down the hallway.

"*Pssssst!*" I whispered.

The cat turned back around and cocked its head.

"We have to wait for the others!" I said.

The cat sat and waited.

There was a push at my sneakers, and I wiggled my way out of the sand tunnel, hopefully for the last time.

I pulled Nabila up, and Ben was next. Gordon was followed by Shane, who was upside down.

"What are you doing?" I asked him.

"I really wanted to try the backstroke through there," he said. "Worked pretty well. You should try it."

"I'll pass," I said.

The cat meowed impatiently.

"All right, all right," I said. "Keep it down. We're coming."

The cat raced quickly down hallway after hallway.

"Left . . . right . . . left . . . ," Nabila whispered, so we could all remember the way we came.

"Someone please slow this cat down," said Gordon. "My stomach's starting to cramp from all the juice and all the running."

The cat finally stopped in front of a wide hallway that led to a dark staircase.

"We'll need to grab torches," I said.

We quickly ran back down the hallway and each grabbed a torch.

When the cat saw that we were ready, it led us down the staircase. The air was cool and moist. There was a single room at the end of the staircase, and as we entered it, we could see an empty floor, and walls covered in beautiful artwork and the bizarre hieroglyphs that we'd seen throughout the pyramid.

The cat padded into the center of the room and sat down.

We placed our torches in sconces around the room and then sat down around the cat in a circle.

The crackling of the torches was all that could be heard.

"So what's next?" Shane asked, finally breaking the silence.

The cat just licked its paw.

"Let me see if these hieroglyphs provide us with any clues," said Nabila.

She jumped over to the closest wall, whipped out her notebook, and began taking notes.

Her *hmmmmm*ing echoed throughout the huge, empty room.

Her pencil scratched furiously on her notepad. We waited. And waited.

I couldn't take it anymore. I was so exhausted, I collapsed onto my side and fell asleep.

## Dem Bones

"Guys, look at this!" exclaimed Nabila.

I woke immediately and jumped up like a crazed marionette. "Have you translated it?" I asked. "Because if not, I'm going back to sleep." Swaying in place, I nearly passed out again where I stood.

I wasn't the only one who had fallen asleep. The others slowly woke up.

"Where'd you get all the energy?" Shane asked Nabila as he yawned.

"I can't see what's going on," said Ben, walking over to Nabila. "We don't all have massive glasses on."

Shane grabbed a torch from the wall and brought it over to where Nabila was pointing.

"This section talks about the 'prince who must not be named,'" Nabila said, getting even more excited. "It must be Murray. *That's* why I had never heard of him."

"Okay," said Gordon. "This was worth waking up for. I just wish my stomach wasn't killing me. Go on."

"It says here," Nabila said, running her hands over the strange-looking hieroglyphs that were half-chiseled into and half-painted on the wall, "that the prince who must not be named was banished from the kingdom after murdering his little brother, a young pharaoh, Amensosa. I *have* heard of him."

"Who was he?" I asked.

"The youngest pharaoh to ever rule ancient Egypt; even younger than Tutankhamen," she said. "Legend has it that he was buried with an army of skeletons to protect him on his way to the afterlife."

"Cool," said Shane. "What sort of swords did they carry? Did they mummify guard dogs to help as well?"

The mummified cat hissed at the idea.

"I'm not sure," she said. "But I do know that he was buried in such a secret location that nobody has found him to this day. Right before I left Egypt for America, my uncle told me that his archaeologist friend, Ahmid, had uncovered a new find that might be the Lost Tomb of the Child Pharaoh. They won't know until they go back next year with the right equipment, but Ahmid really thought he had found it."

"What else does it say about Murray?" I asked.

Nabila kept scanning down the wall, referencing her notes. "His sister remained faithful to him after he killed their brother. Their kingdom imprisoned her, and she died in the pit of a pyramid."

"Could we be in that pyramid?" I asked.

"Possibly," said Nabila. "We could be in Amensosa's tomb, or even someone who ruled after him. The wall doesn't say."

"This doesn't sound like Murray," said Shane.

We all stared at our friend, slack-jawed.

"What?" I said. "Why not?"

"I don't think he would kill his little brother," said Shane. "He loved his sister so much. I just can't see him doing it."

"Ummmm—" Gordon began.

I cut him off. "Did you forget that Murrayhotep has tried to kill us a half-dozen times? What about the whole slave-in-a-mine thing?!"

"He's just got anger-management issues," said Shane.

"Those are some pretty serious anger-management issues," said Ben.

"Um, yeah!" said Gordon, finally finishing his "um."

"There's got to be something else going on here," said Shane. "Something this story is missing. Nabila, are you sure you've translated this correctly?"

"Yes, I'm sure!" she yelled, and snapped her notebook closed. "You're welcome!"

With a HUFF she stormed off to the back of the room.

"I'm taking a nap!" she said. She closed her eyes and immediately began snoring.

Ben and Gordon took her cue and lay down their heads to rest as well.

"Shane," I said. "What is it you see in Murrayhotep that we don't see?"

"First of all," said Shane, "his name is Murray. And we shouldn't disrespect him by calling him Murrayhotep."

"Okay," I said. "What else?"

"We had some pretty deep conversations back at Raven Hill," Shane said. "I don't know if he let his guard down, but he seems like a really nice guy underneath his tough shell. He's just really, really angry at the world. But I don't think it's because he killed his brother. I just don't think he would."

"Do you think you can break through to him?" I asked. "You know—make him change his mind and let us out of this trap?"

"I don't know," Shane said. "If we find him, maybe."

"Something tells me he's going to find us first," I said. "But let's get some rest while we can."

Shane and I lay back down on the dusty ground.

I rolled onto my side to get a little more sleep.

Then . . . "OW!"

Something bit me.

I jumped up from the floor, looking for a scarab, but didn't see anything.

I looked at my side, and a small bit of blood had seeped through my T-shirt. I lifted up my T-shirt and saw a small nick.

I got back down on my hands and knees and blew on the area where I had been lying.

WWWWHHHHSSSSSS!

The tip of a blade poked out of the ground. There was a strange symbol etched into the side.

"*Psst!*" I whispered. "Nabila."

SSSNNNNOOOOOOORACH!

She woke right up.

"What is it?" she asked.

"Look," I said, pointing at the blade. "What does it mean?"

She got down on her knees and stared at the symbol.

Without saying anything, she jumped back up to the wall and looked once again at the crazy symbols there.

"It's Amensosa's symbol," she said. "It's a sword from the skeleton army. I mean, that's the only thing it can be."

"We're in the Lost Tomb of the Child Pharaoh?" I asked.

"There's only one way to find out," she said. She raised her hands over her head. "AMEN-SOSA KHAMUN-RA!"

The sword shot out of the ground, clutched by a skeletal hand.

Roars began to shake the ground.

GRRRRRRRRRR!

Another sword shot up just to my left. I jumped to the right.

"What did you do?" I asked Nabila.

"I didn't mean to!" she said.

"Didn't mean to what?!" I asked.

"Didn't mean to call the army to attention!" she said, jumping as a sword came out of the ground at her feet.

More swords shot through the ground, this time closer to Gordon's sleeping head. Whole skeletons were now dragging themselves out of the floor, which had turned to shifting sand.

"We need to get out of here!" I yelled. "Everyone get up, now!!!"

A skeleton burst out of the sand and held a sword high over Shane.

"Stop!" I yelled, rushing forward. "No!"

But it brought its sword down on Shane.

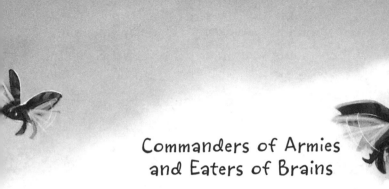

## Commanders of Armies and Eaters of Brains

"Brave soldiers! Halt!" screamed Nabila.

Every single skeleton stopped.

"That was close," said Shane. He shimmied out from under the sword that was an inch above his neck.

"Return to your peaceful slumber," said Nabila.

The skeletons marched into five straight lines of twenty soldiers each. They shuffled their feet in the sand and slowly sank back into place, their swords raised high.

"You will be called upon once again if needed, and the pharaoh is most indebted to you for your service," she said.

Once all that was left were the very tips of their swords, the sand turned into a hard floor once again.

"Whoa," said Gordon. "What was all that stuff about 'brave soldiers' and 'the pharaoh' and 'halt' about?"

"I wanted to try something out," said Nabila. "Anyone can use a charm to wake the skeleton army. Only the descendants of Amensosa's bloodline can command them."

"So that would make you . . . ," I said.

"A pharaoh," said Ben. He bowed down on the floor. "I'm not worthy."

"Oh, stop it!" she said, blushing.

Ben got up and just stared at her. "I'm the luckiest man on the earth."

"Not exactly," I said. "You're trapped with a murderous mummy in a pyramid filled with angry scorpions and hungry scarabs."

"Wow," said Nabila, overwhelmed by the news. "I always thought I was just good at the magic spells. I never thought I was royalty."

"We've got to tell Murray about this latest news," said Shane. "You know how much he loves family."

We all stared at Shane like he had grown a second head.

"Have you gone crazy?" I asked.

"What?" he said defensively. "I'm sure once he has a family member to talk with about his history, he'll feel much better."

"Murderous mummy," I said. "MURDEROUS."

"Who has Murray killed?" asked Shane.

"Let's start with the brains in the jars!" I yelled.

"Those guys were already dead," Shane replied calmly.

"What about his brother?" I asked Shane.

"The hieroglyphs are pretty clear," said Nabila.

"Are they, though?" asked Shane.

"Once again, what about the fact that he's tried to kill us a half-dozen times?" I asked.

"Okay," said Shane. "I agree that Murray has gotten us into situations where we've almost gotten killed. But so has Director Z."

"It's official," I said. "You're crazy. If you can talk Murray out of his plan to remove our brains through our noses or mouths or wherever the next time we see him, please do so. Otherwise, we've got to fight him and find a way out of here."

"Or help the monsters of Gallow Manor find a way in," said Nabila. "I have no idea if I can actually control this army—or if it's even enough to defeat Murray. Chris, you need to eat brain again and tell Director Z to wait near my uncle Omar's shop in Attaba in Cairo."

"How will he know where the shop is?" I asked.

"*Everyone* knows Uncle Omar," she replied.

"And then what?" I asked.

"And then you'll eat brain one more time and talk to my uncle Omar to find out where his friend was searching for the Lost Tomb of the Child Pharaoh," she said. "In the meantime, we'll hide in here with the army, in case we need a little extra help."

"All right, let's do it then," I said.

Once again, we stood in the Chamber of Pickled Brains.

I held a chunk of brain between my fingers. My mouth had already started to feel fuzzy.

"Are you sure you don't want to change your mind?" asked Ben.

"No, I think Nabila's plan is perfect," I replied.

"That's not what I was talking about," Ben said. "I just think this brain might be stronger—judging by its smell, anyway—and I was wondering if you wanted to change your mind." Ben held up a particularly stinky Tupperware container.

"Ha!" said Shane. "Change your mind! That's a good one!"

"No, I think this one is funky enough, and I've already taken a good chunk off," I said. "A brain is a terrible thing to waste."

I looked at my friends gathered around me.

"Maybe this time you can hold on to me and cover my mouth to make sure I don't give us away again?" I asked.

"Good idea," said Gordon.

Suddenly he doubled over in pain.

"Gordon!" I yelled. Shane and I steadied him.

"It's okay," Gordon said, straightening up. "I've just got some insane gas right now."

"So fart," I said.

"I will if I have to," he said. "But I'm just a little worried about what might happen."

"You mean after your thunderburps?" I asked.

He nodded. "Go on, get going," he said.

I plopped the brain into my mouth.

CHEW CHEW CHEW GULP!

Suddenly, I was outdoors. Still standing on sand, but definitely outdoors.

BBBBBRRRRRGLLLL!

I jumped as a creature walked past me. It was huge, hairy, and had two humps.

"Just a camel," I said, happy that I could speak again. "I vonder who I am."

The *V* gave it away. I knew I was Grigore or Vlad. Camilla, also a vampire, didn't have that thick of an accent.

I licked my sharp teeth to confirm. It was at about

that time that I realized I could also see in the dark.

"I like being a vampire a lot more than I like being a zombie," I said.

I looked out at desert as far as the eye could see. I turned around and saw a huge tent. I quickly walked toward it. Last time, the brain had worked for about two minutes, so I only had a minute and a half left.

I moved the tent flap aside and entered. Director Z was sitting at a table with Twenty-Three, the lizard/cat creature from the moon; Gil, the swamp creature; Pietro, a werewolf; Clarice, a banshee; Roy; and Clive the zombie. They studied the map that was lying on the table.

"Ah, Grigore!" Director Z said. "That was fast. Did the scorpions have any intelligence for us?"

"I'm not Grigore," I said. "I mean, I'm in Grigore's body. But it's Chris. You must have gotten my message. The one I yelled through John vhen I vas in his body. How did you get here so fast?"

Director Z jumped up. "It *was* you! I wasn't sure or I would have brought the whole team."

"I don't have much time," I said. "I need you to vait near Uncle Omar's shop in Attaba in Cairo. That's Nabila's uncle. She knows vhere ve are trapped, and thinks he can help you find us. Vait there, and I'll join you again to explain everything."

"Okay," said Director Z. "It was Murray, wasn't it?"

"Yes," I said.

"How are you speaking through monsters?" Director Z asked.

"Murray has a collection of brains that he's—"

"Yeah, yeah," said Gordon. "We know about the brains."

"Ah, man!" I said. "Am I back already?"

"It's okay," said Shane. "There's really no need to cry about it."

I reached up and could feel chunky tears falling down my face.

Before I even touched them, I knew.

"Ew," I said. "Now I'm crying brains . . ."

## The Murder of the Child Pharaoh

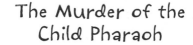

"What are we doing just waiting here?" Gordon asked, frustrated. "Oh man, my stomach is still killing me!"

We sat deep in the Hall of the Skeleton Army, at the very bottom of the Lost Tomb of the Child Pharaoh.

Our bread supply was finished off, and we had all taken turns napping. There was nothing else to be done.

"Let's just relax," said Shane, leaning back against the wall.

"I guess I could go and try to see if the monsters are at your uncle's yet," I said to Nabila. "It didn't take them long to get to Egypt—I'm sure they got to Cairo and found your uncle."

"Okay," she said. "Do they know it's Murray we're dealing with? Do they know his plan with the brains?"

"You mean his hobby?" asked Shane.

"Shane, this is serious," Nabila said. "I've finally translated all of these hieroglyphs, and he's a cold-blooded killer."

"All right, what do they say?" said Shane. "I'm willing to listen. Chris, you can wait just a few minutes to eat some more brain ooze, right?"

"Yeah," I said. "You can take a minute."

I was not looking forward to another All-You-Can-Eat Brain Buffet.

Nabila walked over to the wall to the left of the door and told the following tale:

The Middle Kingdom had come to a close, but before what we now know as the Late Period came a little known, and almost forgotten, era of Egyptian history. Amensosa was chosen by the gods to be the next ruler of Egypt, despite being four years old and the youngest son. But, from the beginning of his reign, young Amensosa faced a perilous life. At the age of six, he was attacked by a crocodile, and nearly lost his life.

"It was my brother," he said as the doctors struggled

to keep the blood in his body.

"What was your brother?" asked the doctors, but the boy pharaoh passed out before he could answer.

The doctors looked at each other strangely, but didn't say anything.

At the age of seven, he was nearly buried inside a pyramid while touring the latest construction.

"It was my brother," he said as workers pulled him out of the rubble, his face pale with fear and covered in the dust of pyramid bricks.

The workers just thought that Amensosa was in shock. They didn't tell anyone what he had said.

Finally, just a few days shy of his ninth birthday, Amensosa was found dead, drowned along the banks of the Nile River.

He couldn't say anything, but the doctors and workers could hear his tiny voice in their heads: "It was my brother."

Suddenly they realized that poor Amensosa had been plagued his entire life by his brother. His brother was brought before the vizier and sentenced to death. Before he could be punished by the most terrible means possible, he disappeared from his prison cell.

"We must find him," said the vizier. "But first, we must make preparations to ensure that our boy pharaoh is properly escorted into the afterlife."

Normally, small clay figures symbolizing soldiers

in an army were placed in the tombs of the pharaohs to ease them into the afterlife. But in this case, it was decided that something truly astonishing had to happen.

One hundred solders who had served under Amensosa were called upon to continue to protect the young pharaoh—for all of eternity.

Under the supervision of a noted magician, the one hundred soldiers were burned to death, and their pearly white, fire-licked skeletons were fitted with weaponry and shields—

Suddenly Murray was at the foot of the stairs. "I haven't heard that tale in a long, long time," he interrupted, clapping slowly at Nabila's performance. "And it's still just as wrong as it's always been. I don't have time to tell you the way things really went. We've just got to get things moving now that I know you children are okay . . . and ready to help the cause."

"We don't want to help your cause," said Nabila. "AMEN-SOSA KHAMUN-RA!"

The earth quaked under our feet. Stronger this time. The soldiers were ready.

"How dare you raise the skeleton army?!" screamed Murray.

The skeletons formed their ranks behind Nabila.

"Destroy the one who killed your pharaoh!" she yelled.

They all stood in place, confused, looking around and scratching their skulls.

"Murray," yelled Nabila. "Kill Murray!"

The skeletons raised their shields and rushed toward Murray.

With a shrill whistle, Murray called the Servants of Horus and a fleet of scarab beetles to attack the army.

My friends and I pushed ourselves against the wall.

The two sides clashed. The Servants of Horus shot electric fire from their staffs, knocking down whole rows of the skeletons. Scarab beetles cracked down on skeleton skulls. Swords came down on scarab beetles, cutting them in half with gushes of greenish-white juice.

Murray was ignoring everything—including us—and was busy collecting the cut scarabs, gobbling down the contents.

"Why is he doing that?" I asked.

"I don't know," said Nabila. "And I don't care. Gordon, do you still need to fart?"

"So badly," he moaned.

"Then bend over and let it loose on Murray," she said.

Gordon bent over and grimaced. Murray had no idea what was coming his way.

Shane pushed past Gordon, bumping his posterior toward the wall, and ran to the stairs.

"Let's get out of here while the getting's good," said Shane. "C'mon, guys!"

"WAIT!" screeched Nabila. "WAIT!"

She desperately tried to point Gordon's butt in the right direction, but it was too late.

FLLLLLLLUUUUUUUURRRRRRTTTTT!

Gordon blasted a chunk of the beautiful wall clean off, blowing rocks into the skulls of a few of the skeletons.

"Yeahhhhh!" said Gordon. "What a relief!"

WHOOOOOSH!

A sword clanged against the wall near Gordon. The skeleton army was not happy.

"Remember your enemy," yelled Nabila, and she pulled Gordon out of the fray.

I couldn't believe Shane had just destroyed our chance to blast Murray away. But he was right that this was the perfect chance to get out of the room, with Murray distracted by the battle.

"We need a room with a door we can shut," I said to the mummified cat, who ran alongside me.

With a *meow*, it shot up the stairs past Shane. Nabila, Gordon, and Ben were just behind me.

As we hit the top of the stairs, I could hear Murray scream, "ENOUGH!"

BOOOOOOOM!

The crunch of bones could be heard.

We didn't have much time.

## Murray's Just Misunderstood

We stood in the room where Kitty had guided us. A lever just to the right of the doorway released a huge stone slab that sealed the entrance to the room.

"Are you sure it can't be opened from the outside?" I asked the cat.

"Meaow," it reassured me.

In the opposite corner of the room, Shane and Nabila were arguing.

"Forgiveness is hard, I know," said Shane.

"It's not hard when someone deserves it," said Nabila. "But Murray is pure evil."

"I disagree," said Shane.

"Disagree or not," said Nabila, "you almost just got us killed. And we could have finished him."

"Guys," I hissed in a low whisper. "Both of you keep it down, or we're definitely going to get killed."

I turned to Shane, angry with my friend. "But she's got a point, you know."

"I just think that we should negotiate with him," said Shane. "Give him a chance. There's something going on with him—some pain deep inside that he's struggling with."

"There's some pain right in front of us that we're dealing with," said Nabila. "And his name is Murray."

"I'm with Nabila," said Gordon. "I wish I could have farted him into oblivion. Then we'd be on our way out of here, and I could get some zit cream." He rubbed his face for a second. "I'm sure Ben sides with her, too."

Gordon gave Ben the eye.

"Well, I . . . ," Ben said.

"Well, you what?" asked Nabila.

Before he could answer, there was a CRASH, and a huge, wet monster roared through the bricks in the back of the room. We stood against the door, stunned.

"It's a hippo!" yelled Ben.

The hippo opened its mouth wide, revealing huge

tusks crisscrossed with river vegetables.

"Ever heard of floss?" asked Shane.

"Back down, Setka!" a voice called through the hole in the wall. "These are still my guests, after all."

The hippo hesitated, but then waddled back through the hole. Once its massive wet butt was out of view, Murray entered the room.

"Hello, children," said Murray. "Thank you so much for being so absolutely stupid as to not kill me. You're clearly not as smart as I had thought. Nope. But your brains are still quite young, and will work hard for me."

"I think it's your mind that we should talk about," said Shane, walking forward. "What's going on in that dusty brain of yours?"

"What do you care?" he asked. "Since the only thing your brains will be thinking about in the very near future is how my acid will be digesting them, I believe the conversation ends here."

"Not really," Shane said, stepping right up to Murray defiantly. "Don't you remember all those games of Go Fish we played in the home under the glow of the spiderweb light? You talked so lovingly of your sister and how much you wanted to be reunited with her."

"Nonsense," said Murray, waving his hand at Shane. "That was all part of my ruse to make you think that I was just as weak as the others there."

"Was it?" Shane asked. "What about the time we

watched *On Golden Pond*—one of your favorites, I might add—and you were so grateful for all the help Director Z had given you?"

"I never lost sight of my plans," Murray said. "Not for an instant. In the back of my throat, I could always taste the brains."

"See," said Nabila.

"Wait," said Shane. "Then how do you explain giving up the home to Zorflogg instead of killing everyone yourself?"

"To gain the immense power of the moon as well as the Earth," Murray responded. "I needed to sharpen the power of the brains. I needed the pure, unrefined monster juice that only the moon could provide."

"And now that you're back on Earth," I said, "you'll just get weaker until we crush you."

"You're wrong," said Murray.

He clapped his hands, and the room filled once again with the sound of unmistakable chatter.

"Oh no," said Gordon. "Not those guys again."

A shiver ran through Nabila's body as a fat scarab scuttled across her shoe.

"He won't bother you for much longer," said Murray. He reached down to scoop up the bug, which chattered happily in his hands. He positioned the scarab so that it was directly in front of his face.

"Your time has come," he said. "And I thank you."

The scarab bowed, and a little drop of monster juice fell off of his mandible onto Shane's arm.

HISSSSSSSSSSSS!

"Ow," said Shane. "It *is* pure monster juice."

With a great crunch, Murray ripped off the scarab's head with his teeth, and chewed happily.

GRIND GRIND GRIND!

The scarab's legs spasmed, scraping off some of Murray wrappings, but he held on tightly. He chewed and smiled, black particles dancing around on his teeth.

GULP.

"Ugh," said Ben, looking green. "I'm gonna—"

"Barf?" asked Murray. "I know, I know. But hold it in a little longer for me. I don't want you to ruin my meal like you ruined yours."

Murrayhotep grabbed a scarab leg that had stopped twitching and ripped it off.

SCHLLLLLOOOOOP!

He stabbed the spiny leg into the dead scarab's body, making terrible squishing sounds.

"*Huuuuurr.*" Ben gagged.

Murray stirred whatever was inside the scarab's hard shell and, with a flourish, pulled out the leg, tilted back the body, and noisily slurped up the insides.

"WHAAAARFF," barfed Ben. "Sorryarrrrfffff!"

"You couldn't have waited a few more seconds?" asked Murray. "This is why I'm removing your brains instead of making you my slaves for all eternity."

Murray threw the empty, but still very stinky, scarab shell directly at my head. I ducked.

"Ha!" he said. "Plenty more where that came from. While nobody was looking, I had these faithful servants scamper into the refinery on the moon and fill up. Figured I'd need a boost once I found my way back to Earth."

"Genius," said Shane.

"Aw, thanks," said Murray. "Hey, wait! Don't compliment me, you little punk!"

"And now I have to thank *you* for the compliment," said Shane. "I always thought I was more of a rocker, maybe even a tad hip-hop, but never punk."

"That's not what I meant," said Murray through gritted teeth.

"We've had some good times," said Shane. "Some for-real good times, you and me, haven't we, Murray? Remember how, after I taught you to play cribbage, you made me my own Senet board so that we could play *your* game? Remember the time we watched *Old Yeller*, and, despite the fact that you're a cat person, we both bawled our eyes out?"

"Yeah, w-well," stammered Murray. "I was weakened and light-headed from the lack of lebensplasm."

"Were you now?" asked Shane as he reached into

his back pocket. "Then how do you explain this letter? It has your signature."

Shane held it up and began to read.

" 'Dear Shane,' " Shane said. " 'I cannot thank you enough for all of the hard work and commitment you have put into Raven Hill Retirement Home. All of the workers here are pretty harsh. Big, stupid Nurses. You'd swear that they had rocks for brains! It's nice to see a young, fresh face around here. After nearly two millennia of running from my own fears and worries, being so drained of lebensplasm, it's nice to be connected to a brain as smart as yours.

" 'You know I can't stop harping on the mind, the importance of the mind, of keeping a level head. It makes me sick to see the demented old farts in this retirement home run into walls, fall over into pools of their own pee, and just generally prove that they have nothing but pea brains (which, I will say, is at least better than the minds of solid rock that those lumbering Nurses have).

" 'Thank you, Shane. Thanks to you and your friends. Thank—' "

"Enough," said Murray. "Clearly, these are the ravings of a lunatic. You all did nothing for me. And clearly, you're not smart, for you to like me despite the fact that I tried to kill you at least a dozen times."

"Aha!" said Shane. "But you didn't. Even you admit you 'tried' to kill us. I think it was because you knew killing us would be wrong. You couldn't do it. I knew you weren't evil, or I would have seen this coming a mile away. We spent so many days together. Remember right after the sussuroblat attack, Chris changed your bandages. It was—"

"I said ENOUGH!" yelled Murray, shaking the room. "Those were the same bandages that *she* unwrapped from me so rudely!" He pointed a bandaged finger at Nabila, and it shook with anger. "I can't even fathom how you got the skeleton army to attack the blood of the Child Pharaoh! And I don't care—it's time for all of you to pay!"

He clapped his hands, and the two Servants of Horus came into the room, their beaks chattering nervously. The massive room still echoed with the sound of Murray's yell.

"What is it with you two?" asked Murray. "Always so flighty."

The two servants looked at each other, squawked a quick conversation, and backed out of the hole.

"And just where do you think you're going?" asked Murray.

Before they could answer, the ceiling above the hole in the wall began to rumble.

A little dust fell on Murray. He looked up just as a massive boulder above his head slid out of place and crashed down.

## Out of the Dust

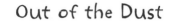

"Murray!" yelled Shane, and he pushed forward, tackling the stunned mummy into the hole in the wall and out of the way as the wall caved in on itself. A massive boulder blocked what was left of the entrance completely.

The pile of rock and dust knocked us back onto our butts, and I ate a sizable sand pie.

The dust finally cleared, but had forced itself into my nostrils. I blew a sandy snot rocket and swallowed hard only to feel a crust of sand sliding down the back of my throat.

"Ugh," I yelled, spitting out a wad of sand-spit. "Shane! Shane?!"

Gordon, Ben, and Nabila all got to their feet.

"What was he thinking?" screeched Nabila.

I ran up to the rocks that had fallen down and pounded on them. "Shane!!!" I screamed. "Shaaaaaane!"

I felt tears in my eyes, but this time they weren't brain ooze. They were real.

I pounded on the wall until my hands began to bleed, and then fell into Gordon's arms.

The cat pawed slowly at my leg and meowed.

"Dude," said Gordon, sitting me down on a rock. "I'm sure he's fine. It looked like he made it through before the bigger rocks fell. All he has to worry about is being stuck with Murrayhotep. And Shane gets along with everyone, remember?"

"I'm not so sure. Murray's probably removing Shane's brain as we speak!" I said. "What do we do? What would Shane do? What would Shane *want* us to do? We have to rescue him!"

"Well, Shane got his wish," said Nabila. "He's finally got some one-on-one time with Murray. Maybe he can talk some sense into him."

"Unless they *were* both crushed," said Ben.

Gordon and Nabila stared at him.

"What?!" said Ben. "Chris is right to freak out! What if we've lost Shane?"

"Wait!" I said. "I know one thing for sure. Shane wouldn't want us to be arguing." I stood up. "Let's get to the Chamber of Pickled Brains while we have the chance. If we're lucky, we'll run into Murray and Shane."

It was deathly silent as we made our way back to the Chamber of Pickled Brains.

Nabila's voice echoed as she called out the way back, "Left . . . right . . . left . . ."

The cat was already in the lead, but it was good to hear her voice.

My brain was numb as we entered the chamber. I had to pull myself together for what was coming next, and I suddenly realized I couldn't do it alone.

"Nabila," I said. "You have to come with me."

"But I thought the pendant—" she started to say.

"I have no idea if the pendant is what brings me to the monsters," I said. "I think the first time I was just lucky, and the other times I was *thinking* about them, you know?"

"Are you sure?" she asked.

"Yes," I said. "I can't think of anyone better to convince your uncle that we're not just a bunch of monsters. Use your pharaoh powers!"

"So how weird does it feel?" asked Nabila. "On a scale of one to ten?"

"The first time was totally weird," I said. "Like, an eleven. You might not even know who you are or where you are at first."

"How am I going to deal with this?" she asked.

"You're gonna be great," said Ben. He was white as a sheet.

"You're not even eating brains," said Gordon. He slapped Ben on the back. "Try to be a little stronger for your woman." He turned to Nabila. "Chris will be there for you."

"He's right," I said. "The first thing to do once you transport is figure out which monster you are. That's really helpful."

"All right," she said. "I'm ready."

"Let's pick out a really funky one," I said, wandering around all of the containers. I caught a particularly putrid whiff from one trash can. "This one. Maybe it will help us stay in our monsters longer."

A really black, oozy brain floated to the top of the trash can. I reached down and plucked off a good-size chunk. Nabila did the same.

"On three," I said. "One . . . two . . . three."

CHEW CHEW CHEW GULP!

"Oh no!" said Nabila. "Why did I do this? I know how brains should taste, and they shouldn't—"

"—taste this way," said Twenty-Three.

I crouched in a dark alleyway, but could once again

see everything. All of the monsters I had seen before were crouched down low with me, trying to blend into the shadows.

"I'm Grigore!" I said. "Yes!"

Nabila/Twenty-Three looked stunned. I grabbed her by her furry lizard shoulders and gave her a good shake.

"Nabila, you're Twenty-Three!" I said. "Ve don't have much time. Look around. Are ve in Attaba?"

"We sure are," whispered Director Z, who walked out of a shadowy doorway. I was stunned I hadn't seen him with my vampire vision. "It's good to see you again, Chris!"

"This way," said Nabila/Twenty-Three, and she burst out onto a larger street.

"Vait!" I said. "Be careful! You don't even realize how fast you are."

I followed her, and Director Z followed me. The other monsters stayed in the alleyway.

Nabila/Twenty-Three skittered right up to a shop and knocked furiously on the door.

"We're closed," said a voice from above. "Read the sign! Or look at a watch! It's midnight!"

"Uncle! Uncle!" screamed Nabila/Twenty-Three.

"Whose uncle?" the voice replied. "Go away!"

"Uncle Omar, it's Nabila!" Nabila/Twenty-Three said.

A light went on upstairs, and then a light went on in the store. The door was flung open, and a man in a dirty tank top with a huge mustache and a terrible case of bedhead stared down Director Z and me.

"How dare you trick me like that?!" he said. "How do you know Nabila? Did you hurt her?"

I pointed down at Nabila/Twenty-Three and said as calmly as I could, "That's Nabila."

"Uncle!" said Nabila/Twenty-Three.

Uncle Omar began to scream his head off.

"EEEEEEEEEEEEEEE—"

Director Z put his hand over his mouth as gently as he could, but Uncle Omar was freaking out. He tried to kick Nabila/Twenty-Three off of his stoop. I bent down to hold his kicking legs in place.

"Listen to me, Uncle," said Nabila/Twenty-Three. "Last summer, when you told that terrible joke about the monkey in a three-piece suit, I was the only one who laughed. Remember? Before I went to America, I told you not to miss me, because I was going to have so much fun telling your joke to all the Americans . . . remember?"

Director Z kept his hand on Uncle Omar's mouth until Omar's eyebrows raised up into his crazy hair.

"It really is you!" he said, looking down. "But how?!"

"I can't explain," Nabila/Twenty-Three said, hugging Uncle Omar's leg. "Just remember what I'm about to tell you."

"Okay," he said, patting Nabila/Twenty-Three's head. "I still miss you, by the way."

"You need to let these two gentlemen know the location where your friend Ahmid is looking for the Lost Tomb of the Child Pharaoh. They desperately need to get there. My friends and I are trapped inside. I will tell you why later, when I'm myself again."

Uncle Omar looked back up at Director Z and me, and was terrified once again.

A half-transformed werewolf was running right for the store, snarling.

I faced the werewolf head-on, grabbing its heaving shoulders as it tried to smash past me and into the store.

WHAM!

Vampire strength coursed through my body, and I was able to hold the werewolf in place.

"Pietro!" I yelled. "What's gotten into you?"

"I have," growled the voice.

"Murray?" I asked.

"You better believe it!" growled the werewolf. He reached up to my head and squeezed it hard.

"GO. BACK," said Murray/Pietro. "Get your sweet little brain back to my pyramid where it belongs."

"Chris!" yelled Nabila/Twenty-Three.

She jumped up to claw at Murray/Pietro's face, but his grip only got tighter.

I blacked out.

## Murray Tells It Like It Is . . .

I woke up with a gasp.

Nabila did the same, but with a scream. I tried to grab her, but she was rolling around like crazy, clawing at the sand.

"Chris!" she screamed. "Don't let him hurt Uncle Omar!"

I grabbed her and held her in place on the sandy ground.

"Nabila!" I said, shaking her.

"Nabila! It's okay! I'm here. We're back now."

She screamed like a banshee and then locked eyes with me.

"You're back," I said as calmly as I could.

"What happened?" she croaked. "I'm not even sure I convinced my uncle to help."

"Murray took over Pietro," I said. "Murray must be alive."

"Right you are," said Shane, and he leaned down to help me up while Ben and Gordon helped Nabila.

"Shane!" I yelled. "You're alive!"

A small tear started to run down my cheek, but I wiped it off quickly and gave my friend a huge hug.

"I thought you were dead," I said, squeezing him hard before letting him go.

"Nope," he said. "Murray actually cushioned my fall. See, he's a nice guy after all."

"But you weren't able to talk him out of destroying us and the rest of the world?" I asked.

"Nope. I'm still working on that," he said. "But he did say something strange about having to choose between his brother and his sister. And I did get to spend a little more time with the serpopard. I think it'll actually come if we call it. Now, the bird-heads are going to need a little more work . . ."

"Why didn't he kill you?" asked Gordon.

"As a thank-you for saving his life, he's letting me

die with my friends," Shane said.

"Where is Murray now?" Nabila asked, wiping the brain-boogers that were streaming out of her nose.

"Over there," said Shane. He pointed to the back of the room.

Murray swayed in place, guarded by the two Servants of Horus.

"Why aren't you oozing brain?" Ben asked me.

"I dunno," I said. "Maybe that only happens the first few times."

"It's terrible," said Nabila.

Suddenly Murray snapped back into his body.

"Outta my way," he yelled at the Servants of Horus, pushing them aside.

SQUAWK! SQUAWK!

He stormed right up to me, grabbed me by my shirt, and spat into my face.

"How DARE you spoil my brains!" he said, overcome with anger.

"Your brains?" I said. "You mean the brains that you stole?"

He threw me to the ground and turned back to the brains.

"These brains are not stolen. They stole from me," he roared. "They stole my kingdom and destroyed my bloodline. These are the brains of my enemies, eternally trapped for vexing me!"

Murray gripped a jar and held it high. The brain inside trembled with fear.

"How did they *vex* you, exactly?" Shane asked. "We didn't have a chance to talk about that when we were trapped together under the rocks."

"Well, I guess since I'm about to remove, pickle, and eat your brains," Murray said, "I can tell you."

"Well, that's nice of you," said Shane.

"Don't make me change my mind," he said. "I'm only doing it so I can taste your fear later."

"Got it," said Shane. "Zip it."

"When my brother was attacked twice and said, 'It was my brother,' he was trying to tell people that I had saved him. He wasn't saying I was trying to hurt him," said Murray.

"I KNEW it," said Shane.

"SHUSH," everyone in the room said.

"I wrestled a crocodile to the ground for him," Murray continued. "I held back the largest rock that would have crushed him at the pyramid site. But after he died, those gossiping doctors and workers kept mentioning 'It was my brother' over and over. Everyone assumed that I had killed him, that I was upset at my father for making my younger brother the pharaoh, that I was hungry for the throne. I couldn't convince them otherwise.

"After everything I had done for my brother, the

aristocracy not only accused me of his murder, they ended up creating a new dynasty. The kingdom should have been mine. MINE!!!

"I was so angry, I ran. I escaped from the grasp of the new, false pharaoh, only to see my brother truly destroyed when they removed his brain. Just like they removed the brain of my sister for defending me. And they didn't even give them a proper burial. My brother was never entombed in this useless shrine.

"The vizier doomed my siblings to eternity in the spirit world to punish me. I could only choose one of them to bring back, because only one member of a bloodline can be resurrected by another, and I was the last, the only one. They forced me to make an impossible choice. If I brought one back, the other would be cold and alone in limbo.

"I let them go. My last memories of them were seeing them as brainless, drooling mummies. That's when I realized that my ancestors were wrong—the brain is where the real power lies in humans. The seat of thought. The house of our soul. I knew that gray matter should be revered just like the liver and the heart—even more so.

"So I plotted my revenge.

"I turned myself in to be executed, but before I did, I paid off my mummifier. He left my brains in, and when he mummified me, I was given eternal life *and* eternal brains, not just eternal life like all of those brainless mummies! I went through all the records and erased my name—"

"That's why Murray never sounded like a mummy's name to me," said Gordon. "It was never a mummy's name."

"It was the greatest name of anyone ever to be mummified in the history of mummification!" screeched Murray.

"You shouldn't interrupt him," I said.

"Right," said Gordon as he avoided a swift slap in the face from Murray.

"I crept from tomb to tomb," said Murray, "swooping in and stealing brains from the dead pharaohs—all the false leaders—before the mummifiers could remove them.

"I was collecting the brains in order to tap into their powers. After the end of the dynasties, I collected them all in this room and created herbal concoctions that drew out their powers. I never realized that I would be able to use their powers for Second Sight, to jump into another body and control it. But after I mistook one of the chunkier concoctions for my morning fruit smoothie, the brains' true power was revealed.

"If I could perfect these powers, I could control the leaders of the world—the presidents, the prime ministers, the generals of armies. With the world's leaders under my control, I would have a much easier time coming to power, first in Egypt, and then throughout the world.

"And now, your young brains will add the perfect flavor to my mind-control mix, which I was perfecting before my unfortunate detour at Raven Hill."

"You mean you were a traitor even at Raven Hill?" Gordon hissed.

"Who do you think controlled the monsters once they were covered in membranium on Paradise Island?" replied Murrayhotep, looking at Gordon as if he were a bug. "I just used the membranium as a cover—and it worked!"

"But you were terrified of Zorflogg!" Ben said.

"Zorflogg was a numskull," Murrayhotep growled, and spat on the floor. "There are greater forces at work in the monster world. I am one of those greater forces, and I have guzzled enough monster juice to dominate the world. Zorflogg was my tool. He merely provided the opportunity for me to unfold my plans. He weakened the monsters that would be my most powerful enemies. You see—"

"Ow," I yelled, and clutched my stomach.

"I'm not finished yet," said Murray.

"Chris," yelled Ben, pointing at my pant leg. "What's happening?"

I looked down to see brains oozing out of my pants.

"Gross! Brains are coming out of your—" Shane started to say.

"You sick little child," said Murray. "How dare you continue to desecrate my sacred room?"

The feeling of the brain ooze dripping down my leg was overwhelmingly disgusting, and I could feel a big chunk working its way down.

"You're the sick one," I said, and I kicked the chunk at Murray as it started to come out of my pant leg.

It hit his chest, but not with a SPLAT.

It made a metallic JINGLE sound and fell into the sand.

Murray reached down and picked up my pendant. "Well, well, well," he said. "What do we have here?"

"No wonder it hurt so much," Shane said. "Brains weren't the only thing that came out of your—"

"Give it BACK," I screamed, lunging crazily at Murray.

"Be happy that it's just your brains I'm removing!" Murray responded. "If this hadn't tumbled out on its own, I would have carved you up like a Thanksgiving turkey in front of your friends!"

Murray clapped his hands twice, and the Servants of Horus pointed their staffs at us.

"Take them to the Brain Removal Chamber!" yelled Murray. "I'm finished with them." He placed the pendant around his neck. "Taste you later!"

## Brain Removal
## Chamber

"So, do you still think Murray is a good guy?" Gordon asked Shane. He pulled at his leg and arm shackles, but it was no use. We were chained tightly to the wall.

"I have an idea," said Shane. "I've just got to figure out the best time to bring it up with Murray."

"Uh-huh," said Gordon. "Sure. Yeah. Yep."

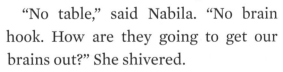

"No table," said Nabila. "No brain hook. How are they going to get our brains out?" She shivered.

"There's nothing in here," said Ben.

"Not even sand," I said. "Except for what's left in my sneakers."

I wiggled my feet and could hear the shifting sand.

"Maybe the bird-heads brought us into the wrong room?" wondered Ben.

"Just give me a minute," I said. "I'm sure I'll come up with a plan. I've got to get that pendant back."

"Let the pendant go," said Shane.

With a great BOOM, the huge iron door swung open again, and the Servants of Horus dragged in—

"Neferkare!" I yelled. "No!"

"Don't worry about me," said the dusty old mummy. "I'd be more concerned about you."

The bird-heads tried to push Neferkare down, but he pushed back with a growl.

SQUAWK! SQUAWK!

"Get off of me!" Neferkare yelled. "I've heard enough about this cursed room to know what happens next. Give me some dignity."

He lay down on the cold stone floor.

"There," he said. "Now I'm ready."

The servants dragged chains from all four corners of the room to shackle to Neferkare's arms and legs.

They left the room and closed the door.

"Well, it looks like we're not going to be able to rot away together for all eternity after all," snickered

Neferkare. "Oh well. I was getting sick of being so old and tired. Maybe my brain will finally feel energized again before getting devoured by that madman."

The sounds of CHITTER CHATTER SKITTER SCRAPE came through an opening at the bottom of the large door.

"More scarabs?" asked Gordon.

"Get ready for one heck of a show!" yelled Neferkare. "Come and get it!"

A river of tiny scarabs poured into the room and rushed over to Neferkare, covering his head.

He spat and yelled, "I hope you choke on my brains, you little—AH, AH, AAAAHHH!"

One by one, the scarabs disappeared from his bandaged face, and Neferkare's twitching stopped.

"Where are they?" asked Nabila.

"Neferkare!" I yelled.

He sat upright and opened his mouth.

BLLLLLLARRRRG!

He barfed up the river of tiny scarabs. Each one held a tiny chunk of gray matter in its jaws.

They swarmed over to the door but didn't leave.

"Neferkare?" I asked. "Can you hear me?"

He turned to me and opened his mouth.

"Haaaaaaaaaah," he hissed. "At last I diiiiiieeee!"

He fell back and turned to dust.

POOOOOOF!

From the large door, there was a great HISSSSSCLICKCLICK, and a massive beetle entered the room, along with a powerful stench.

"Ugh," said Gordon. "It's a giant dung beetle!"

"Actually," said Nabila, "all scarabs are dung beetles. This one just happens to smell."

"Do you have to be right even when you're about to die?!" screeched Gordon.

The swarm of tiny scarabs CHITTERED an evil little hello and then piled up the brains behind the dung beetle. When they were all finished, the dung beetle began pushing the brains into a ball with its hind legs, rolling it around the chamber.

SQUISH SQUISH SQUISH!

"Well, now we know why there's no sand in the room," said Shane. "Gotta keep those brains clean."

The scarabs helped replace fallen bits of the beautiful, juicy brain as the dung beetle rolled it around the room. The ones that were finished helping chattered hungrily at us.

"Something tells me we don't have long," I said, gulping. "What are we going to do? We've got to *use* our minds before we *lose* our minds."

"RA-SET-RA-DUNN!" Nabila screamed, and she flicked her hand.

Nothing.

"I think you made them angrier," said Ben.

Shane began to whistle.

WHIS-WHIS-WHISTLE-WHIS—

"'Iron Man'?" I asked.

"Just go with it!" he said. "Everyone!"

Ben and I joined him.

"I can't whistle," said Gordon.

"Just hum," I said.

WHIS-WHIS-WHISTLE-WHIS—

"Why are we even doing this?" asked Nabila. "We have to come up with a real plan."

The scarabs were done, and the dung beetle rolled the brain even faster around the room, packing it good and tight. It looked something like a real brain again.

The scarabs rushed at us.

"All right, all right!" yelled Nabila, and she started to whistle.

The scarabs skittered back and forth over our feet, trying to decide whose brain to pick first.

WHIS-WHIS-WHISTLE-WHIS—

The scarabs gathered on my legs.

"LOUDER," I screeched.

WHIS-WHIS-WHISTLE-WHIS—

They rushed up my pants, their little legs digging into the fabric.

"Chris, no!" Nabila screamed.

They swarmed my face.

I screamed.

# Chris Loses His Mind

The scarabs skittered all over my face, pushing into my eyes, my ears, and my mouth.

I squeezed my eyes shut and blew the scarabs out of my mouth.

My friends continued to hum, scream, and whistle "Iron Man." But I could barely hear them behind the mask of writhing bugs.

They CHITTERED and SCREECHED, and pushed into my nose.

BOOOOOOOM!

The room shook, and the scarabs fell off my face.

"It's working," yelled Shane.

We were thrown forward as the rock wall crumbled.

I spat out the last of the scarabs and turned around to see the serpopard bound into the room.

The dung beetle let out a frustrated SCREEERRCH and quickly rolled Neferkare's brain out through the door. The serpopard bounded toward it.

"Wait," said Shane. "Can you get us out of these shackles?"

The serpopard hesitated and then turned around.

It leaped to Nabila and brought its hairy snake head down on her shackles.

CRACK! "Ah!" CRACK! "Ah!"

"My hands are free!" yelled Nabila, and she was able to unshackle her own legs.

With several more CRACKs, we were all free.

"Let's get out of here," I said.

"Show us the way," Shane said.

The serpopard shook its head.

"Why not?" asked Shane.

It turned to Nabila and bowed down.

She walked up to it awkwardly and touched its snaky head.

"Show us the way," said Nabila.

The serpopard jumped up, crashed through the

door, and ran down the hall.

"Hurry!" I yelled.

We followed the serpopard, winding madly down hallway after hallway, into rooms, up stairs, and finally out into the blinding desert sun.

"Nooooo!" yelled Gordon. "My face is melting."

"Cover your eyes," said Shane. "Open up your hand, one finger at a time."

"I feel like a vampire," said Nabila.

We couldn't see anything, but we could hear a huge roar from below us.

I slowly peeled my fingers away from my face and saw that we were halfway up a pyramid, the blazing blue sky above, and a huge mass of shifting figures hundreds of feet below us in the desert. They were gathered between the pyramid and a huge river.

"Is that the skeleton army?" asked Shane.

"Looks like it," said Nabila. "That must be the Nile River."

"Oh man, those scarabs are the biggest ever," said Gordon.

Thousands of cat-size scarabs clashed their massive jaws together.

SNAP SNAP SNAP!

Monster juice dripped out of their mouths.

Wild dogs howled. They scampered and snapped in the hundreds.

"Jackals," said Nabila.

Huge, tank-size hippos slammed against each other.

"What are they doing?" asked Ben.

"Getting ready for battle!" said Shane.

"It's a twisted, sick army," said Gordon.

"And there's its twisted general," I said, pointing down at Murray, who stood in front of the masses.

He was flanked by the Servants of Horus.

"The world is ours!" he yelled at his army of skeletons, jackals, scarabs, and hippos.

A great roar of approval lifted into the sky.

"The world is ours," he repeated. "We just need to take it. And today. Today is the day we begin!"

ROOOOOAAAAAR!

"We are at our most powerful," said Murray, and he held an object high in the sky.

The bloodstone reflected the sun into my eyes and made my head explode with anger.

"The pendant," I yelled. "MY pendant!"

Without thinking, I ran down the rocky slope of the pyramid, screaming like a lunatic.

"GIVE IT BACK TO ME!"

The only thing in the world I wanted was the pendant. It was all I could see.

Halfway down, I was jerked to a stop.

"Get off of me!" I yelled, trying to rip Shane's hands from the neck of my T-shirt.

"Who cares about the pendant?" he said. "It's not worth it if your brain is chewed up and rolled into a ball by the scarabs."

"I care about the pendant!" I screamed as Shane dragged me back up the side of the pyramid. "You don't understand. You haven't felt its power."

I had to push Shane off of me and retrieve my pendant of power before the others helped him. I clawed at his hands.

"We escaped from the Brain Removal Chamber without it, didn't we?" yelled Ben, slamming into us and almost pushing us off the edge.

"Come with me," I said, pushing off of the rock.

But Gordon grabbed me with a meaty grip.

"Dude, chill," he said. "You're frothing at the mouth."

I shook in my friends' arms as we hung on to the very edge. Down below was my prize.

"I know I'm crazy," I moaned. "I want it so bad, though."

My friends waited to see what I would do. Shane rubbed my back.

"We need to stop," said Nabila as calmly as she could. "We need to come up with a plan."

All four of them surrounded me and slowly pulled me off of the edge.

The serpopard stared at us as we retreated into the dark, cool pyramid.

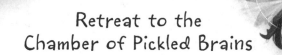

# Retreat to the
## Chamber of Pickled Brains

"I'm so sorry," I said to my friends.

I put my hand up to my face. My head hurt. But it felt good to be back in the pyramid.

"It's okay," said Shane. "It must have been exhausting to keep the monsters from eating each other on the moon. And all the brain adventures you've taken . . ."

"My brains feel like a sussuroblat in a Barfitron," I said. "I feel like I went from being the leader to being a dung beetle."

"A dung beetle who can roll up a mean brain?" asked Shane.

"Nope," I said. "Just a regular old turd."

The roar of Murray's evil army could now be heard even deep within the pyramid. A little sand shook off of the bricks above us and settled on our hair.

"Well," Ben said, "at least we know everyone's still outside. What are we going to do?"

"Let's destroy the brains!" said Gordon. "Crush all the containers and let them ooze into the ground."

"Then Murray won't be able to use them!" I said.

"That's an excellent idea," said Ben.

"I'll just take one more bite so I can see where the monsters are," I said. "And then we'll finish off Murray and his army."

"Wait!" Nabila said. "I've got a better idea!"

"What could be better than destroying the brains that Murray can use to take over the world?" Gordon asked, but Nabila just ran out of the small room we were hiding in and down the hall.

We rushed down the hallway to keep up with her.

"Nabila!" I yelled. "Careful! We're not even sure everyone's outside! What if we wake up the scorpions?"

She ignored us, and we ended up in a room we had only spent a few seconds in before.

Nabila was already inside, holding up a beautiful, long robe.

"Hurry, put this on," she said to me.

"What is it?" I asked as I quickly put it on and wrapped it around my body.

"An Egyptian priest's robes," she said. "Here!" And she handed me a staff and hat.

"Why?" I asked.

"I need you to present the brains to the army," she said. "I think it might sway them into helping us."

"Wait," I said. "What?!"

"Just do it!" she said. "I'll explain on the way to the brains."

We ran through the hallways to the Chamber of Pickled Brains. Nabila laid out her master plan.

"I can handle the skeleton army because I'm a descendant of the Child Pharaoh—"

"Oh, my queeeeeen!" said Ben.

"Keep movin'," yelled Gordon.

"—but I think we can control the other sections of the army, too," she continued. "Each pharaoh had a special connection to an Egyptian god, and each god has a special connection to certain animals. If we find the right brains, and they're presented to the army in a respectful way—by a *hem-netjer*, or ancient Egyptian priest—it might sway the scarabs, jackals, and hippos to join us and turn against Murray!"

"How do I do that?" I huffed. The robes and hat were hard to run in.

154

"You'll have to hold up and ceremoniously present each brain until we get the attention of the animals," she said.

"But there are dozens of brains in there," I gasped. "How do we know who is who?"

"Maybe we could ask them?" said Shane.

We finally reached the entrance to the Chamber of Pickled Brains . . .

. . . only to find that it was gone.

"Wait!" I gasped. "What happened to the door?"

Nabila ran up to the wall where the entrance had been and felt the stone there.

"Murray must have sealed it up," said Nabila.

"He's one thorough mummy," said Shane. "Very organized. Before preparing your army, close your brain door."

"Oh, shut up," said Gordon.

"What are we going to do?" asked Ben.

I stepped up to the stone and raised my staff high.

"Open," I said. "Open the waaaaaay!"

Nothing happened.

"Nice try," said Nabila. "But I think we're just going to have to wait until Murray opens the door again."

"But the next time he does, the army could be ready to advance!" said Ben.

"We'll have to tackle him as soon as he opens the door," said Gordon.

"Something tells me that's not going to be easy," I said.

"We can hope the monsters show up before then," said Ben.

"We don't even know if my uncle was able to give them the right directions," Nabila said.

"And I can't nibble on any gray matter to find out," I said, knocking on the wall where the door should have been. "Ow!"

"Wait, now I've got an idea," said Shane. "Where's the serpopard?"

"You lost the serpopard?!" yelled Gordon. "Rule number one of pyramid survival: Never lose your serpopard."

"First off, it's everyone's serpopard. Second, look what I found in the last room," Shane said, holding up a new recorder.

"Sweet!" said Ben.

TOOT-TOOT-TOOT-*tut-tut-tut-tut* . . .

TOOT-TOOT-TOOT TOOT-TOOT *tut-tut* . . .

"'Happy'?" I asked. "What happened to 'Iron Man'?"

"We don't want the serpopard to show up all angry, do we?" asked Shane.

TOOT-TOOT-TOOT-*tut-tut-tut-tut* . . .

The serpopard came down the hallway, and Shane stopped playing.

"Get over here, quick!" Shane yelled.

The serpopard approached. It towered over us.

"I forgot it was so tall," said Ben.

It leaned down and gave Shane a big lick with its forked serpent tongue.

"Aw, thanks," said Shane. "Here's the deal. We're waiting for Murray to open the door to his brain room. As soon as he does, tackle him, and we'll head inside. But just tackle him—don't hurt him. Got it?"

It nodded its snaky head.

"Now we wait," I said.

"Maybe not," whispered Nabila. "Look!"

The light of bright torches came down the hallway toward us.

# Bag Them Brains!

We ducked into the small room across from the Chamber of Pickled Brains.

I lay on the ground and peeked around the corner.

Far down the hallway, Murray's figure appeared with the Servants of Horus.

"We'll bring a handful of brains with us to Cairo!" Murray yelled. "Once we've secured that city, and I've made every world leader ignore the crisis, we'll come back, load up the rest, and head off on our World Takeover Tour."

Suddenly one of the Servants of Horus fell to the ground and was dragged back by a large figure in the shadows. He didn't make a single SQUAWK—Murray and the other servant didn't even notice.

"Something's happening," I whispered back into the room.

The second servant was quietly dragged into the dark. This time I recognized the figure.

"It's Roy!" I whispered. "The monsters couldn't have waited two minutes?! Now Murray won't open the chamber! How are we going to defeat the army?"

"Maybe we won't need to anymore," said Ben.

Murray got to where the door should have been, and I crawled back into the shadows.

*Pleeeeeeeease*, I thought. *Open that door.*

Murray put his hands up to the wall and chanted, "THOTH-RA—"

HOOOOOOWWWWLLLLL!

"Jackals," said Nabila.

The sound of barking, scraping, and fighting came down the hallway.

Murray turned to see where the sound was coming from, and was startled.

"You!" yelled Murray.

Director Z walked up to Murray, grabbed him by his shoulders, and held him in place.

My friends and I walked out of the room, followed by the serpopard. Down the hallway, crazed jackals snapped at Twenty-Three, Roy, Pietro, and Clarice. Grigore slammed one in the head with a closed fist as it jumped up to snap at him.

FLOOOOP! It hit the sand.

Pietro glanced at Clarice and nodded.

"HOOOOOOOOOWLLLLSCREEEEEEEEEECH!" they yelled together.

The jackals put their tails between their legs and ran.

"Tell the others to prepare for battle!" yelled Murray as they whimpered down the hall.

"It's time for you to come home," Director Z said. "You're in a lot of trouble, old man."

"I'm not old anymore, Zachary," Murray said, now grabbing Director Z by the shoulders. "And you're the one who's in trouble. Give me back my guards, and maybe I'll let you walk out of here."

"Let him go, and maybe I'll let you walk out of here," I said, pointing my staff at Murray.

Murray looked at me and laughed.

"You somehow survived my Brain Removal Chamber," Murray said, "and instead of fighting for your life, you're playing dress-up."

"Enough," said Director Z. "We're done here."

"Yes," agreed Murray. "Yes, we are."

He flung Director Z into the monsters and lunged at me, grabbing my staff.

"Let me show you how to use this thing," he growled.

But before he could snatch it out of my hand, the serpopard slammed into him, and both of them crashed through the wall into the Chamber of Pickled Brains.

When the dust cleared, I saw Murray crawling out from under a large pile of rocks.

The serpopard was struggling to get up, too stunned to notice Murray was about to get away.

We surrounded the doorway to make sure Murray couldn't get out.

He backed into a corner and grabbed a Tupperware container of brains.

"What's your move, mummy?" yelled Gordon.

"Always have a trapdoor in your brain room," he said. "Always."

Murray turned around and pressed a brick further into the wall.

FLOOOSH!

He fell through the sandy floor.

"NO!" I yelled, and rushed into the room. "We've got to catch him!"

The trapdoor swung back up.

I frantically pushed the brick Murray had pushed.

Nothing happened.

"He's got what he needs for the big battle," I said.

"Now we need to rush to grab the brains we need."

"Brains?" asked Director Z.

"We'll explain later," I said. "It's what's going to save us."

"I would hope so," said Director Z. "I thought we were here to save you."

"What are we going to put them in?" asked Shane, ignoring Director Z.

"We need something worthy of a pharaoh," Nabila said, looking around. "Canopic jars . . . or a ceremonial bowl?"

Nabila was taking too long. I bit my tongue and let her take her time.

"Or we could just use the plastic bags you have in your fanny pack," said Ben.

"Fine," said Nabila, pulling out plastic bag after plastic bag from her fanny pack. She had dozens.

"Why do you even have those?" asked Gordon.

"We use them when we take the werewolves for walks," said Ben. "You usually need three or four to collect all of their—"

"Ooooh," said Gordon, getting it.

"We should have enough for all of the brains," said Nabila, passing them around. "Let's just bring them all."

"Make sure to add a little brain ooze to each bag. It's probably best to keep them a little wet," said Shane. "Look, I found this rusty old spoon to scoop some up."

We were bagging up brains like crazy, but it was taking a lot of time. We had to wait until they bobbed to the surface to snatch them, or we'd be elbow-deep in brain ooze.

"We've got to hurry before he mobilizes his forces," I said.

"We've only got one spoon, Chris!" Gordon snapped.

When we were done, each of us held a dozen brains in bags, and they were heavy.

We rushed to the door, but before we could run out of the room—

CHITTER CHITTER SKITTER SCATTER!

"Oh no," Gordon said. "Scarabs again?"

# Get Out!!!

"Nope," said Shane, peering out of the doorway. "Scorpions. A parting gift from Murray."

"Quick," Nabila said to me, "try out some of the brains on the scorpions."

"What do you mean?" I asked.

"Just hold up a bag and tell them to bow down!" she said, and handed me a brain. "Everyone, this might take a while, so do what you can to keep them from coming into the room."

Director Z shot me another confused look.

"I promise," I said, "I will explain everything to you once I get a chance."

A sea of scorpions washed up into the hallway in front of the door, their hard bodies cracking against each other. Poison dripped off of their tails. Their pincers clicked together.

Shane handed me a bag, and I held it high. "Bow down to your all-powerful leader."

Nothing.

Pietro turned into a wolf and used his powerful jaws to snap at any of the scorpions that tried to rush into the room. The other monsters and the serpopard joined him up front.

Another bag. "BOW DOWN."

Nothing.

With quick, tiny CRUNCHes, Twenty-Three ate the scorpions when they got too close to me or my friends.

"Earth food is delicious," he said.

"You're livin' the dream, Twenty-Three!" yelled Shane.

I was handed a new brain. "BOW DOWN."

Nothing.

"We can't hold them back much longer," roared Roy. "There are just too many."

I raised brain after brain. Roy was getting stung

like crazy as he tried to knock the scorpions away from his face.

"Arrrgh!" he yelled, and he finally fell over.

The scorpions rushed forward.

SKITTER SCATTER SKIT.

"Chris!" Nabila yelled. "Hurry!"

But she was too close. The scorpions covered her, their tails lashing down.

Shane ran forward, but it was too late.

Nabila screamed.

"Noooooo!" yelled Ben.

Gordon handed me a brain.

"Bow down to your leader!" I screamed.

The scorpions stopped.

Nabila burst out of the pile that covered her.

"Ah," she said, pulling three scorpions out of her hair and tossing them to Twenty-Three. "I almost got stung a few times. I'm okay."

Everyone stopped and stared, first at the scorpions, and then at me.

"No time to waste," I said. "Everyone ready?"

Everyone nodded.

"Let's do this," said Shane.

"Nabila?" I asked.

She looked confidently at me. "I'm ready."

"To battle!" I yelled at the scorpions, raising my staff high. "Murray the mummy would destroy your leader.

We cannot let that happen. We must meet his army in the open desert. Are you ready?"

The scorpions chattered what I could only assume was *yes*.

"Go now!" I yelled. "It's time! Out of the pyramid to battle."

The scorpions rushed out of the room, and we followed them, with the serpopard in the lead.

"Hold on to your brains!" I yelled.

A few twists and turns later, we came to the entrance halfway up the pyramid. Grigore stood on the inside of the entrance, with two staffs pointed at the Servants of Horus. They all jumped when they saw us.

"Wait!" I yelled, and the scorpions waited at the entryway.

I ran past the servants to look outside. I was ready for the bright sun this time and shielded my eyes. Murray's army was already up along the river, marching north.

"Hurry, Shane," I said, rushing back in. "Work your magic."

Shane walked over to the two bird-heads. They twitched nervously.

"I vouldn't do anything you might regret," said Grigore, raising the staffs a little higher. The tips glowed a magic electric blue.

"They're fine," said Shane, casually stepping up to them. "Right, guys?"

SQUAWK! SQUAWK! SQUAWK!

"Look," said Shane. "We all know how Murray's been treating you. Not very well, right?"

SQUAWK!

"Join us," Shane said. "We've already got the scorpions and the serpopard on our side. And a direct descendant of Murray's bloodline."

"Hi," said Nabila.

The Servants of Horus bowed down to her.

Director Z said, "Is Nabila a—?"

"Later!" I said to Director Z. "Hurry, Shane."

"Guys, c'mon," he said. "Are you in?"

SQUAWK!

"Give them their staffs back," said Shane.

Grigore gave him a funny look.

"It's okay," I said.

Grigore handed back the staffs, but hissed, revealing his sharp vampire teeth.

"Looking good," said Gordon. "Those are the sharpest I've seen yet."

"Thank you," said Grigore. "I feel pretty strong. The strongest I've felt in centuries!"

"So does Murray," I said. "And his army is on its way to Cairo as we speak. We've got to stop him before he puts his plan in motion. You two"—I pointed at the Servants of Horus—"help Nabila take back control of the skeleton army." I pointed at the serpopard. "You come with me and my friends—we'll head for the scarabs. They looked like the largest section of Murray's army. You've got to defend us while we choose the right brain. Everyone else needs to hold off the jackals and the hippos. Understood?"

"Understood!" everyone responded.

Gordon snickered.

"What?" I asked.

"You really do look silly in that outfit," said Gordon. "It's hard to take you seriously with that little hat."

"Gordon, if you want to get back to your sports, do what I say," I said. "Everyone line up outside the entrance."

Everyone, scorpions included, headed out into the light. Shane pulled me aside.

"Chris, before we get started, can I make a request?" asked Shane.

"What is it?" I asked.

"Tell everyone that they can't hurt Murray," he said. "If we make it through this, I still want to talk with him about everything. Plus, I think he's more valuable to us alive than he is dead."

"Shane," I said, "I still don't get your obsession with Murray. But I trust you."

We walked out into the light.

Crowded on the stone outcropping were the very agitated scorpions, the serpopard, and all of my friends and monsters. We were ready.

"All right," I said. "Let's do this. But listen closely—we take Murray alive, understood?"

Everyone nodded.

"Get his attention," I said to Clarice.

She opened her mouth wide and let out a bloodcurdling SCREEEEEEEEEEEEE!

The army stopped its advance.

Murray, just a small white figure up against the Nile, slowly turned to me. I couldn't even make out the outline of his mouth from this far, but I could hear his voice clearly in my head.

"Just DIE already!"

## Battle Royale

Murray stared deep into my eyes. His army of scarabs, jackals, hippos, and skeleton warriors turned and roared. Their angry breath kicked up the sand. The serpopard wiggled its forked tongue in the air in disgust.

When the dust settled, I raised my staff.

"Surrender now, Murray!" I yelled. "It would be the best thing for everyone."

Shane walked over to my side. "And all you others," he yelled, "a breath mint is suggested. The worst part of that little sandstorm wasn't the sand."

"Let's get serious," I whispered to Shane.

"That breath was serious," Shane replied.

My staff still raised, I continued to speak. "We already have the scorpions and your servants under our control. And now some of the fiercest monsters from North America and the moon are ready to do battle for us."

"Those bird-heads are useless," Murray yelled. "And there's a reason I left the scorpions back at the pyramid. I can handle those Gallow Manor goons. What else ya got?"

"Nabila!" I screamed, and she stepped forward.

She raised her hands, and now the sand that had blown up into our faces blew back into the faces of the army.

"AMEN-SOSA-KHAMUN-RA!" Nabila screamed so loudly that the pyramid shook. "Brave soldiers, surround Murray! Protect your pharaoh!"

When the dust cleared, the skeleton army stood around Murray in a circle three lines deep. The closest ones pointed their swords directly at his head.

"How is it possible that you're listening to this little brat?" Murray growled. He held up his hands in surrender.

"I am an heir to the throne of Amensosa," said

Nabila, "filled with the light of Ra, the wisdom of Thoth, and the relentless drive of Horus."

"Unbelievable," said Director Z.

The monsters nodded in approval.

"I knew there was something special about her," said Clarice.

"Wow," said Ben. "I really am the luckiest man alive."

"Impossible!" said Murray. "This must be some of that phony magic that you've cast at me before. I am the last of my bloodline! They took away my birthright and the birthrights of all the pharaohs who were never able to fulfill their duties. That is why I fight today—nobody is ever going to give you anything. At best, they're going to take it away!"

Murray quickly moved his hands from above his head to his sides, sending a shock wave of sand through the skeleton army.

"Now rise up and follow your true leader," Murray screamed, and the army fell in line.

"This is going to be harder than I thought," said Nabila.

"Let's get to it!" I yelled. "CHARGE!"

The scorpions rushed down the side of the pyramid, and we followed behind them, screaming. The brains in the bags sloshed around crazily.

As soon as we hit the sand, Murray's army rushed toward us.

The monsters and Director Z headed for the hippos and jackals. Nabila and the servants headed directly toward Murray and the skeleton army.

I kept the scorpions on course for the scarabs.

As soon as their hard bodies met, I screeched to a halt in the sand, hoping that we would find the right brain soon. My friends handed me brains as fast as they could, as the serpopard stood ready to defend us.

I held one high. "Bow down to your leader!"

SCRAPE RATTLE HISS CRUNCH!

The scarabs didn't stop their forward momentum. Their drooly pincers swiftly cut scorpions in half, spewing monster juice and scorpion guts into the sand.

I held up another brain. "Bow down to your leader!"

To my right, Roy slammed another hippo to the ground.

BOOM!

Grigore jumped on the hippo and tried to drain it dry, but before he could, there were more hippos behind the fallen one, and they charged.

Another brain and another and—

"Ah!" yelled Shane. "That scarab just cut off my shoelace!"

"Watch your toes!" yelled Ben. He jumped up and pounded a scarab into the sand.

"Maybe hold up a few brains at the same time?" asked Gordon.

"It will probably just confuse them," I said.

Two brains and three eaten shoelaces later, I still didn't have control of the scarabs. Shane was karate chopping the scarabs that were making it past the scorpions. Their monster juice squirted everywhere.

"HUH!" CRUNCH!

"HUH!" CRUNCH!

"Hand Ben your brains!" I yelled at Shane.

I looked over to see Nabila and Murray, battling almost head-to-head, each commanding a small section of the skeleton army. More of her army had fallen, and the bird-heads were nowhere to be seen, but she had picked up a sword and started hacking away along with the skeletons who were left, stopping from time to time to throw a spell at Murray.

CRACK—off came a skeleton head.

"You should have followed me!" she screeched.

I held up more and more brains, but none of them were working.

"Maybe you need to say something different for the scarabs," said Ben.

Before I could figure out what that "something" should be . . .

"ROY! GRIGORE!" someone screamed. "Director Z is hurt!"

I looked up to see Director Z on the ground, surrounded by jackals. Pietro was trying to keep them away, but there were just too many.

Roy and Grigore ran to help, and the hippos turned toward us angrily.

BWWWWWOOOOOAAAR!

"We can't even deal with the scarabs anymore," yelled Shane. "I'm slowing down. The monster juice is starting to soak into my clothes and sting my skin."

Three more brains and nothing. There were almost no scorpions left. The serpopard was struggling to keep scarabs from snapping our legs (or our brains) in two. It moved forward to fight the scarabs.

"We're running out of brains," I said. "One of them has got to work!" I held another up high. "Bow down to your leader!"

Nothing.

The hippos charged directly at the serpopard, knocking it down. They turned to face my friends and me, mouths open wide. Breath worse than one hundred rotting fish washed over us, and I got woozy.

"I wish hippos were just big, stupid cows," said Gordon.

BWWWWWOOOOOOOAR!

Brain number thirty-two. "Bow down to your leader!"

Nothing. The scarabs kept skittering. The hippos kept blasting us with their breath.

"Grigore! Roy!" I yelled. "Anyone!!!"

The hippos galloped toward us at full speed.

The river receded from the shore and then rose up terrifyingly high.

"Wahooo!" yelled the wave.

"Clive!" I yelled, pointing at the zombie surfer.

"Better back up, my dudes!" he yelled, staying perfectly balanced atop the monstrous wave. "This bad boy's gonna have one killer curl!"

There were dark figures just below the surface of the wave.

"Zombie sharks!" yelled Shane. "Back up, back up, back up."

"Don't drop the brains!" I yelled. We rushed as fast as we could away from the riverbank. "And don't forget which ones we've already tried on the scarabs."

The scarabs and the last of the scorpions followed us. The hippos just stood there, dumbfounded. Murray was nowhere to be seen.

"Waaaa-hoo!" yelled Clive. "Hangin' TEN. Yeah!"

CRASHBLURBLEBLURBLECRASH!

Almost all of the hippos were swept away into the river, but one washed up right next to us.

It stumbled out of the waist-high water and went right for Ben.

BWWWWWOOOOOOAR!

The hippo was just about to lock its jaws on Ben's head, when a zombie shark shot out of the receding water—

CHOMP!

—and dragged it back into the river.

We didn't even have time to think before the scarabs attacked again.

The serpopard was still one hundred feet away, and we were surrounded.

"Brain me!" I yelled, and Gordon tossed me a brain before being knocked over by the scarabs. He bounced on top of their hard shells, missing the SNAP-SNAPPING jaws by inches.

"Bow down to your leader!" I screamed.

The scarabs ground to a halt.

Gordon pulled his finger out of a half-closed scarab jaw.

"Awesome timing," he said, and rolled his way over to Shane, Ben, and me.

The serpopard finally made it back to us and put its head low to crack a few scarab shells.

"Wait!" I yelled. "They're with us now!"

The serpopard stopped.

There was another scream coming from the jackals.

"Director Z," I said, and turned my staff on the scarabs. "To the jackals. Run them out of the desert!"

The SNAPPING and CHATTERING started again, but this time it wasn't for us. The scarabs rushed toward the jackals, snapping off tails and chewing on paws.

"AAAAAAARRRRGH!" I yelled, and my friends joined me.

The jackals scattered, and the scarabs followed them.

Once the dust cleared, I could see Roy helping Director Z. His leg was a chewed-up, bloody mess, but I could already see he was going to be okay.

"Well, I guess you ended up saving me after all," said Director Z.

"I haven't saved anyone yet. We still have a little more work to do," I said, and I pointed to my right. With only a few members of her skeleton army left, Nabila was struggling to defend herself against Murray, who was slashing furiously at her.

"We've got to hurry," Shane said.

"Everyone, NOW!" I yelled, and we rushed toward her.

CLANG! CLINK! CLANG!

"THOTH-DUNN-KHEFER-RA!" Murray yelled, and Nabila's sword flew from her hand.

We were only fifteen feet away now.

Murray looked right at me, raised his sword, and brought it down on Nabila.

# The Blood
of Amensosa

"Waiiiiiiiiit!" yelled Shane, and Murray stopped.

Nabila looked at Shane with relief and happiness.

The skeleton army (well, the dozen soldiers that were left) stopped and stood there, totally confused.

"You don't want to do that," Shane said to Murray.

Murray raised his sword high again.

"You're right!" he said. "I'd rather take her hostage. Now back off."

"Listen to me," said Shane. "You're

taking your own bloodline hostage. You're ruining the only chance you have to see your brother and sister again."

"I still don't believe you," he said. "I wrestled control of the skeleton army from her easily. Like candy from a baby."

"Well, you do have three more millennia of experience," said Shane. "She didn't even know her true power until earlier today."

"Back off!" said Murray again. He positioned the sword against Nabila's neck.

"Shane, maybe you should back off," said Nabila.

"Amensosa had no sense of smell," Shane continued. "Nabila has no sense of smell."

"Prove it!" Murray growled.

"She never would have survived the trip to Paradise Island in the sea worm if she had a sense of smell," Shane said.

"A ruse," said Murray.

"She would never be able to date Ben if she had a sense of smell," said Shane.

Murray seemed momentarily startled, but composed himself and said, "Maybe. Go on. What else ya got?"

"You," Shane said, pointing at one of the soldiers in the skeleton army.

The skeleton jumped, surprised to have someone talk to him. He slowly turned his head to Shane, his neck bones creaking.

"You have sworn a solemn oath to protect Amensosa and only take orders from those related to him," Shane said. "Is that true?"

The skeleton nodded.

"And is Nabila an heir to the throne of Amensosa?" asked Shane.

The skeleton nodded.

"This poor soldier has no brains," said Murray. "And as you know, I don't think very highly of people who don't have any brains. Speaking of which, give me my brains back. We're headed back to the pyramid now. Isn't that right, Nabila?"

I looked at the bags of brains in my hands.

I looked over at the serpopard and the other monsters. Roy helped Director Z hobble into place, his pant leg bloody and sandy.

"I just don't believe you'd kill her," Shane said. "I used to only *think* that you wouldn't kill her. Now I know."

"Give me the brains NOW!" Murray yelled, and the point of his sword cut just a little bit into her neck.

"Shane!" she screeched.

"You've never killed anyone," said Shane. "If anything, you've wanted to give people the gift of life. Your sister and your brother."

"Don't bring them into this," Murray said.

"I know you're angry because the vizier forced

you to spend three thousand years contemplating an impossibility. How do you choose one sibling over the other? And it's only gotten worse over time. What would they think of your actions now? But now you don't have to choose. And it's time you faced both of them."

Everyone stared at Shane.

"Nabila, as a descendant, can bring the other one back. So tell her how, and if it doesn't work, you've got a hostage, and we back away. And if it does, you stop this madness and turn yourself in."

Murray slowly lowered his sword.

"If it doesn't work, I swear on the spirits of my ancestors that I will kill you all so quickly that you won't even realize you're dead."

"Fair enough," said Shane.

"Shane!" yelled Nabila. "This is a lot of pressure."

"No it's not," said Murray. "Either it works or it doesn't. You just have to chant a spell." Murray pointed at my staff. "Give me that thing. And for Pete's sake, take off that robe."

I handed him my staff. I left the robe on.

"Hold on to it with me," he said to Nabila. "Say what I say, but with Amensosa's name."

They gripped the staff.

"T H O T H - D U N N - A N U B I S - D U N N - R A - MURINDA-RA!" Murray said.

"T H O T H - D U N N - A N U B I S - D U N N - R A -AMENSOSA!" Nabila said.

The wind blew, and two tiny tornadoes began to spin in front of Nabila and Murray. The rest of us backed away to keep the sand from blowing into our eyes.

The tornadoes pulled up to reveal . . .

"My beautiful brother! My wonderful sister! It's been so long!" Murray got on his knees as the two mummies approached. "I missed you both so very much!"

"Then what took you so long?!" said Murinda-Ra. "You could have brought me back from the spirit world, and then I could have brought Amensosa back when I got here! You were just so clouded by anger, you could never see that."

"Really?" asked Murray. He crumpled into the sand and shook his head. "I've been terrible."

"Terrible, angry, grumpy, pigheaded," said Amensosa, helping him up. "We've been watching you. You've been crazy."

"I know," Murray said, starting to weep. "I just missed you both so much, and it's been so long."

"Admit it," said his sister. "You were kind of into the mind control. You had forgotten about us. As soon as your love for us left, you were just a tool of your own anger."

"I know, I know," said Murray. "I'm so sorry. Don't be angry with me!"

Murray now openly wept into his hands.

"We most definitely will be angry with you," said his brother. "But that doesn't mean we don't love you!"

"Yeah, come here!" said his sister, and she and Amensosa wrapped Murray in a bear hug.

The three of them cried with joy, and then Murray looked over at Nabila.

"I should have known we were related the first time you unraveled all of my wrappings," said Murray. "Come here and give me a hug."

Nabila gave me a strange look and then walked into their arms. They squeezed her tightly, and everyone giggled.

One of the soldiers dropped his weapon and started to clap his skeletal hands together.

CLICK CLICK CLICK!

The others joined in, and then the rest of us applauded as well.

I high-fived Shane.

"Take off the robe," said Gordon.

"All right, all right," I said. "It's getting hot, anyway."

I finally pulled off the hat and sweaty robes that had helped us win the battle.

"Man," said Gordon. "I could use some shade."

"To the pyramid!" yelled Amensosa.

We headed to the pyramid.

Must. Go.
SOUUUUTH!

"So that's what happened after Murray hijacked the ship," I said.

"And here we are now," said Director Z. His bandaged leg was propped up on a chair.

"I think it's kind of harsh that we're making Murray spend the next millennium all cooped up in this tomb," said Shane.

"Yo, you know what was harsh?" asked Clive. "The way the wave slammed on those hippos—BAM! So gnarly!"

"Thanks again for that," I said.

"Don't thank me," Clive said. "Thank the zombie sharks. They can get some killer waves movin' when they get to groovin'."

"I'm glad you were right about Murray," I said to Shane. "But I still think he needs a little time to think about what he did."

"He's got a lot of catching up to do with his siblings," said Nabila.

"Well, I'm glad it's not me who's going to be in here for a millennium," said Gordon, pacing. "I've got softball practice to catch up on."

"Yes, well, funny thing about your absence," said Director Z.

"What?" asked Gordon.

"Principal Prouty and Lunch Lady have been able to keep people from missing you at school, but—"

"But?" I asked.

"But there has been an interesting development in each of your homes," Director Z finished.

"What?" Shane asked.

"Your parents started to get lonely at home and kept forgetting that we'd told them you were still there. They started to peek into bedrooms. They started asking strange questions around town. We had to start using fresh tactics."

"What sort of fresh tactics?" I asked. "Will they even remember we're their kids?"

"Oh, we're not doing anything to them," Director Z said. "They're much easier to control now that Nurses have replaced you at home."

"What??!" I asked.

"Yes, it's much easier to believe the kinds of lies we're planting in your parents' heads if someone physical is there to represent you."

"My room!" moaned Gordon. "Who is it—Nurse Inx? He's probably already broken my bed."

"We've also had to extend this lie into your school for the sake of your parents. Nurses have assumed each of your identities there as well."

"My perfect grades!" moaned Ben.

We were interrupted by a huge BOOM and HISS.

The serpopard ran past the Game Room, hissing, followed by Kitty, who was clearly chasing it.

"Watch out, you buffoons!" yelled Murray from the hallway.

"I'm sort of happy this whole situation didn't take away his grump," said Shane.

Murray walked into the room and right up to me.

"I thought you were in the basement," I said.

"I was until I realized I owed you something," he said, and held up my pendant. "I'm really sorry about stealing this from you. And for everything I did."

I grabbed it and held it up to the light. "Thank you," I said.

I put the pendant around my neck. Almost immediately, I had the insanely powerful sensation that I needed to get out of the pyramid.

Gordon walked over to me. "When we get home, I think I'm finished with the monsters. I've got to focus on my sports. I can't concentrate when people are trying to eat my brains. The stress is too much. Look, I have two more zits! I—"

"Wait," I cut him off. "I have to go."

"Go?" asked Director Z. "Where?"

"Just on a walk," I said. "Yes. A walk south. I must walk south."

I marched into the hall and ignored the serpopard as it chased Kitty back down the hallway.

"Chris," Shane yelled from the door. "Where are you going?"

"I. Don't. KNOW," I was barely able to say, so excited at the prospect of getting out of the pyramid and walking—no, running—south.

South.

South.

Go, go, go!

"Chris?!" Gordon yelled. "This is serious. I mean it. CHRIIIIISSSS!"

# ABOUT THE AUTHOR . . .

M. D. Payne is a mad scientist who creates monsters by stitching together words instead of dead body parts. After nearly a decade in multimedia production for public radio, he entered children's publishing as a copywriter and marketer. Monster Juice is his debut series. He lives in the tiny village of New York City with his wife and baby girl, and hopes to add a hairy, four-legged monster to his family soon.